I0627949

Acknowledgement

Because spirits don't like their picture taken

A body double was used...

It is "Bubba" of Flora Mississippi

Bubba is in a long term relationship with "Yeti." The couple has two

people. Lisa and Chris. The two people have four children.

DOG GONE DUMAS

by - *Jack Robertson*

OTHER BOOKS BY THIS AUTHOR

TRILOGY OF ANGELS SERIES

VIGILANTE SPIRIT

CLONE AND ANGELS

ANGELBOTS

This is a work of fiction. All characters and events portrayed in this book are products of the authors imagination and are used fictitiously.

You may order Dog gone Dumas at Amazon.com (Kindle)

Dog gone Dumas/ John Chester Robertson

Third Edition

ISBN: 978-1-7322684-7-0

Registration number: TXu 2-338-480

Contents

Introduction

When Dumas was just a young working dog, a wandering spirit boosted this dreary duck retrievers' intelligence. That caused him to hate his job. Realizing his plight he rebelled against his master. And then he was angry with everything in his life. To make matters worse he knew the angels were calling him *Dumb ass*. And he agreed because his life was just a miserable series of dumb dashes into a dirty swamp. So he deserted.

And all heaven broke loose…

After dangerous adventures and misadventures he found a happier home and a great family. He went from being regarded as not very smart to being heroic. The same angels who ridiculed him soon decided they love him. Dumas is their favorite animal.

While angels live forever, his time to pass came…and went. On an impulse an angel offered Dumas the choice of passing normally in the manner of living creatures . Or, to become a spirit. As unthinkable as it seems Dumas chose to be a spirit.

This is how things turned out…

1

Dumas spirit

Soft breezes carry him in soft and gentle arms. Nothing impedes his flow over the valley into new hopefully wonderful challenges. Dumas is as happy as a bird. Perhaps even as one of his favorite ravens. The strength he felt moments ago when he launched his existence on the plane of a spirit rather than a stiff corpse proves he's made the right decision. Abruptly he's alerted that far below something terrible is about to materialize.

A police sergeant arrives home without suspecting anything out of the ordinary in response to a call from his bride of a mere six months. He walks into the bedroom suddenly aware he's walked into an unthinkable trap. She's about to pull the trigger of the gun she's pointing at his heart. He's staring down the barrel of a short 38 special when suddenly something distracts her. Dumas has launched himself at her arm. While he can't move it the pressure he exserts against it creates enough force to throw her off of target. Her intended victim was her husband Mark..

It is just enough time for him to draw his service weapon. He pops a round directly between her fingers. *"Why did you do this?"* He demands to know. Through screams of pain. *"I never loved you!"* *"You are nothing more than the death benefit on that life insurance policy I made you take out!"* *"Now you took that away from me!"* She clams up. This wasn't a part of her scheme.

Dumas can't believe this mess. As the lawman readies his weapon to finish her off, Dumas commands to his conscience *"Stop!"* Horror and pain drain from the mans' face. Instantly he relaxes. Sergeant Mark returns to the professional he's always been. It's over. *"She's just another criminal who tried to murder me." "What's new?"*

The abruptly estranged husband croaks into his mike reporting the situation. *"I have just prevented a murder...Whose? mine."* A police wagon comes screaming down the street.

After what seems like an eternity the door opens. He tearfully surrenders both his and her weapon to another lawman. Dumas is satisfied but bewildered. He realizes that he tipped off the lawman and distracted the killer. Just how and why? For this innocent victim, an officer of the law life will go on.

A car waiting just down the street for the would be murderess pulls away. Her partner in the deed deserts her leaving the wretch to fend for herself. She wouldn't ever look back if she had a choice. She doesn't have one. They will each try to pin it on the other without a shred of loyalty.

After a bitter pause during which he will become nearly insane with grief and sadness. He knows something stopped him from vengeance. It's too soon to think about. An angel smiles upon the spirit from above. *"You did well."*

Dumas thinks affecting this rescue was way beyond his ability to make things happen. Even if he is the highly enlightened spirit of the dog whose life was once a pathetic duck retriever. And even as the cherished third member of the family in a big Elkridge house on the hill. A home where he was called Dumas. Named that after famous Alexandro Dumas, author of *The Three Musketeers* by his grateful master and mistress. *"How did I do that?" "I'm only a dumb ass dog."*

Dumas doesn't really like even this more dignified name. Because it sounds too much like the one given to him by a mischievous spirit and continued by angels. *"Dumb ass"* certainly wasn't a very nice thing to be called.

So he has some relief in being named after someone so significant as Alexandro. Still, it could be better. But he can't imagine anyone calling him something nice. Especially any who knew him before he passed and chose to be a spirit. But his adventures have just started.

"Hi Dumas!" he hears from somewhere out over the horizon. Happily, he recognizes the voice. It's Hiker his second master. Dumas is thrilled. He hasn't seen Hiker or his old mistress since before they died in an accident. *"Just want to say old buddy we really appreciate the way you looked after our son Lorenzo and his family after we were gone."* Dumas just smiles and thinks he's wagging his tail. Spirits don't have tails. Of course his tail, backside it was attached to, and his other living animal parts are buried up on the hill alongside of the house. But then just beneath the thin layer of soil his old tail does stir a bit.

They each pause quietly for a moment realizing although they lived in the same house for many years this is the first time the dog could ever speak to his old master. It is a wonderful moment. However sensing his uneasiness, His old master is the first to speak.

"Now that you are with us again Angela and I have something that you can help us with …. if you are willing?" Dumas tries to be nonchalant but can't. Anything involving Hiker and Angela, the other two members of their three musketeers trio, is the best thing that's happened to him in years. *"We needed your help in looking after our missing twin." "You not only located him but just saved his life."* Dumas tries to speak but just nods mutely.

Then realizing that Dumas thinks once more the three musketeers, Hiker, his wife and he will work together again, Hiker adds softly, *"Of course we won't be here because we've gone to a better place."* At last Dumas responds in a clear voice. *"Please tell the mistress I love her."* Hiker's voice fading in the distance. *"I will,"* Hiker *promises, then chuckles, "Don't steal any ducks!"* Dumas slyly lies. *"I promise I won't!"*

Lorenzo was the only child Dumas is aware Hiker and Angela had. Neither he nor Mark his twin grew up in the big house. Both were secretly sent off to live with relatives of Hiker. Everyone in the house was at risk. Danger was severe from many sources. A vengeful maternal grandmother, foreign adversaries and evil demons repeatedly tried to destroy the family. Hiker's family never were very close to one another. Even so one element took Lorenzo in for a time. An even more distant relatives took in Mark. There was love but it was without passion as is the case with many.

The cousins who took in Mark rarely if ever spoke to or of Mark and Lorenzo. No one got around to telling Mark he is a twin. Or even that they were not closely related. Just the same they raised Mark with consideration and kindness. Anything more was none of their business. To them he was their son. Lorenzo and Mark have little in common except both are good souls and if Mark shaves his beard they would look alike.

Lorenzo's foster family really were too busy to care for him. So he found his way back up the hill to his biological parents early. At least he knows who he is. Poor Mark took his distant cousins as brothers and never realized his twin existed. After high school Mark enlisted in the Air Force. After his honorable discharge he came home to become an officer of the law. It was a profession he learned in the military. And he's excellent at his job.

He met this evil gold digger online. She and her female accomplice have a stronger relationship than the husband and wife. Under questioning this so-called friend claims it was all of the wife's idea to bump him off for his life insurance. Mark knows only his miserable witch wife point the gun at his heart and pulled the trigger.

Now there isn't any evidence to substantiate her whining plea she was the masochistic tool of a dominating wretch. Only she is charged, convicted and sentenced. In 20 years, less time off for good behavior she may be released. It will be after her youth has faded, That's assuming she survives prison. Charges against the accomplice will be dropped after negotiations.

An investigation discovers this person who claims to only be their maid although Mark never met her. She is in the country on an expired visa. And strikes a deal to leave the country after her attorney surrenders a stash of Marks' money the woman has pilfered. Of course it was less his fee. Mark is poorer but wiser.

"Maids here don't earn salaries in six figures," fumes the District Attorney. Reluctantly her offer to return the bulk of the money and leave the country is accepted. Authorities don't want the public here to know one of their officers of the law was so naive. To the DA, the word of

the wife, one who would have been the murderer, doesn't seem to be a very good witness against her accomplice. Mark agrees because he needs his money. An angel quips, *"At least he thinks he needs money."*

Dumas doesn't care one way or the other about the entire matter. He's having a difficult time. Just existing as a spirit has its' problems. He tries to scratch behind his ear. Hiker observes from afar. Fallen angels are delirious with laughter at this wanabee spirit. A loyal angel points out the need for a gyro. *"Not going to happen." Bad enough to invent spirit dogs without modifying the spirit,"* says another.

Without a firm grip on anything solid he just spins out of control. The spinning stops only after Hiker orders from a distance *"Sit!"* Although he can't actually sit, his rotation slows, and his trajectory stabilizes. Of all places he doesn't care to be, he is floating over the municipal dog pound. With barely the slightest nudge here and there

Dumas sets the entire population of the facility free. They escape in every direction like their lives depend on getting away. It does.

After receiving multiple dire threats, Evil Marta, the disloyal coconspirator to Mark's attempted murder decides living here isn't good for her. She pays Mark back then evil Marta finds her way back to the island where she was born. It isn't good for Marta there either. But it's her home. She won't wander again.

Nothing is the way it was when she left there either. That's because her childhood friends have discovered golf. They'll never completely regain their sanity. Nobody yells *"Fore!"* to let anyone know a golf ball is in the air. That would spoil the joy of smashing one another in the head with the ball. Or tripping anyone trying to play through with a putter. Her neighbors are vicious. And Marta's happy to be home.

Back at Mark's police station, even though he was proven to be the victim by his mysteriously activated lapel camera, he is still restricted to desk duty. He's bored. But things will become very busy for everyone soon. An incredible situation unfolding in the strangest place, a school for gifted young engineers. Something weird is going on there late at night.

A call comes into the station. Mark orders the dispatcher to have the two night shift cars in the area of the school to check it out. On several nights recently the caller saw strange lights near the closed building, as recently as last night. Mark thinks, *"It would have helped if they reported it when it happened instead of waiting,"* " *Well, better late than never."* Mark isn't the only one with a problem.

Poor Dumas tries with all of his might to negotiate the casual weightless ease of other spirits who fly, float and hover. It's extremely strange to be up here with the ducks instead of retrieving them from a pond or stealing them from some hunter. He develops a new appreciation of flying critters, except fleas which he remembers with disgust and still despises. Although he cannot be mistaken for a duck and shot down by a hunter, Dumas doesn't fly where they shoot.

He idly reminisces *"I wonder what became of my old boss Hunter after I ditched him?" "I think I'll check him out.' "Maybe I can teach him to fetch!"* Instead of looking for trouble he finds himself at the police station with Mark again. He hasn't the slightest inkling why.

" Mark, we all sympathize with your situation and thank God for the fact your lapel
camera was on or you'd be sitting behind bars in one of those cells back there." "But we can't have an officer out on the street so soon after engaging in a shootout with his wife." "You are on the front desk for as long as we feel it's

necessary." The sergeant nods respectfully. And mumbles *"Thank you Captain."*

But Mark's not under any illusion. If the only witness to this event wasn't his lapel camera he might easily have been indicted, tried and awaiting sentencing. Even so, in one way or another he's still in the jailhouse. He's not angry with his superior officer who just wants to be prudent in case Mark wigs out over how close he came to biting the bullet.

As unlikely as it appears, if his estranged non-spouse somehow pulls a rabbit out of a box and manages to challenge the evidence then Mark's an instant collar. Dumas takes it all in and tries to give the Captain a paw in the style humans call *the finger.* But soon realizes. a paw's just a paw and a finger is the real thing. And the two don't mean the same thing at all.

Dunas dog spirit wonders why he's feeling loyalty to someone he's just met. Then he is shocked to realize, except for a beard, Mark's face is identical to Lorenzo's, his most recent master. *"But this isn't Lorenzo...hmm." "It all makes sense now!" "Wow!"*

2

Free wheeling

Dumas spins uncontrollably high over the city. A familiar voice scolds. *"Dumas you dumb ass, why are you trying to move like you're still mortal?"* Dumas slows to a wobbly roll looking all around. The sound of the being is unmistakable, but Raven's shining black beak isn't to be seen. Dumas scolds back, *"You know I only let my very best friends call me dumb ass, don't you?" "I bite everyone else."* No further conversation is needed to let each know their good natured kidding is OK. The friendship is intact.

The Raven isn't any more visible than was Hiker. Both are within a more heavenly dimension. While Dumas isn't totally within the world of the living neither is he close to theirs. So, he stops to take stock of who he has become and where he exists. He understands his spirit world doesn't come with an instruction book. For the time being he's bouncing around like a kite trying to catch a breeze.

Upside down and looking away from the earth he stops trying to move. His spirit being hallucinates. Momentarily he feels as though he's floating over a green meadow. No longer just a dog with a strong body, now one with all of his senses and intellect. His awareness is omnidirectional. His hearing and perspective are vastly more sensitive. Spirits and eagles are kinsmen, each to its' own way.

His old doggy hunger that led him to steal and eat ducks and skunks is long gone. He's in an element of consciousness where only the present moment matters. Almost like a normal dog. But like many before him he finds himself wondering *"What now; what's next?"* The answer is obvious. It doesn't matter. Self is obsolete here in this in-between dimension.

Eventually his mind settles down and he opines that things do matter after all. Yet it was good to think that nothing matters if for only a moment. Nothingness isn't anything but it's relaxing. Something attracts his attention.

He spots a strange and interesting sight down on the ground. Four horse vans pull onto a large parking lot beneath him. They precisely park next to one another. And each is numbered. First they line up perfectly, as though upon command. From each a white unicorn steps smartly out, stopping at a numbered starting point. A silent signal is given. Then each beautiful steed sets out on its' own way seeking a path through an intricate maze. It is up to each unicorn to find the only one to some mysterious exotic wonderful prize at a golden spot in the middle.

As each prances with its' single horn held proudly high in a stately manner, Dumas realizes they have merely virtual bodies. Then the first into this winding maze is blocked and crumbles into dust where it stands. A foggy boohorn jeers. *"Loser!"*

Reappearing with its beautiful white mane flowing the refreshed image trots back into the van it left. Each van drives off disappearing one by one. At last just one competitor is left. Without reason Dumas cheers it on. And when this unlucky unicorn fails to find its' way and it crumbles as did those before, Dumas is crushed.

When the last van pulls out, in its' wake the parking lot dissolves. A young gamer turns to look at no one he can see and complains *"Dude you ruined my game!" "At least one always wins!" "Put up more money or get lost."* Then without a word the gamer also disappears. Dumas realizes this complainer is just a part of the game. This time Dumas is flabbergasted.

" *Is everything in the world just a humongous game?"* Dumas shrugs in revolt. *"My spirit will not be wasted on games!"* A sage old ghost warns, *"You never know whether you're only a pawn until the final game is over." "Go learn who's running the game."* Dumas thanks him and sets his mind to do just that. Hearing this the Raven warns, *"BEWARE! "Maybe you don't want to know."*

Dumas wonders whether he's a player or just another pawn.*" As a tiny puppy I was kidnapped from my mom and brothers and sisters soon after I was born." "Then I found myself sitting in a cabin with a man who just used me to fetch ducks." "That's why I was always stealing their ducks." "What do I know of this world?"*

"I know enough to be afraid of being the only dog spirit in the world living a virtual existence." And as an afterthought, *"... and never trust humans."* Raven squawks, *"Really?"* He replies, *"Ok, most humans."*

Frustrated with his inexperience as a spirit, Dumas pretends he still has a body and plods down the center of a busy highway. No one's there. He notes with satisfaction that if he is a living creature that an eighteen wheeler would run over him. Smiling to himself, *"Now it feels really great to be a spirit!"* He hasn't the slightest idea where he's going but knows he's getting somewhere. *"This is awfully slow."*

"Let's try something else."

So he imagines he's a raven. It works. But with his doggy brain he forgets and tries wagging his tail. This sets his raven body into a tailspin. Once again Dumas is spiraling out of control. He does rolls and head over tail. Once he calms down then he gets the hang of flying like a bird. Landing silently Dumas takes off and sails away gracefully like a balloon. He's proud of making it onto the roof of a railcar then looks to his friend Raven for her opinion, but she's gone. She's not actually gone but doesn't want anyone else to see her talking to the *"worst dog gone bird ever in the skies."*

The tracks carry the train west past places he heard of but has never been. *"I'm going somewhere new."* One sign says *Buzzardville* another *Wallow*. And he passes both without leaving the comfort of the slowly rolling car. Gradually those wheels roll well out of populated areas into more of a wilderness. A sense of tranquility flows within.

These shining rails move his train into curves and bends and always along rivers. Dumas is still interested in the ducks he sees but doesn't budge. Now satisfied he's mellow enough for real adventures. Although he's still as a raven, Dumas sails away from the train car to a mountain. He's been here before.

It is where a gentle God loving old lady was living. Her name and reality were *Grace.* She lived alone in her mountain cabin and mostly survived off of the wilderness harvest, plus the few garden staples that can grow in rocky mountaintop soil. Something is wrong!

Dumas doesn't really know Grace because she wouldn't have taken to a talking dog. He recalls seeing her when he was sent on a mission. One to rid her mountain of some threatening demons. But he knew even then she was the mother of his first master. It was a hunter known by the very name *Hunter.* As much as Dumas would like to get to know this saintly soul, she isn't in his future. For the simple reason Grace is Hunter's mother. One whose leg he chewed a bit too hard.

Then pushed Hunter off of a pier yet rescued him. And worse, left him behind for good. There's no love between the two of them. Plus, he almost destroyed her other son Mal.. It doesn't get better. And now that she's dead Grace knows everything he has done.

He knows she's a good person because the angels want him to keep her safe until she's ready to transit. Both of her limping sons and their families have cabins nearby. They didn't understand her loss of strength due to aging nor her need for their help. Grace never complained. She struggled on every day with a prayer on her lips. Grace loved her Lord. She drove her old car to chapel weekly. It never really ran as well after she ran over Buck, her son Mal's criminal cohort. Grace blew off suggestions she buy a newer jalopy. *"It may sound funny, but it always gets me back and forth."* It didn't use much oil because she didn't give it much.

Back on the Elkridge hill Dumas's earthly body lies half buried. Three angels, Lucien, Ralph, Roman and another, the Grim Reaper, gather around the remains of the dog's carcass. Another stands nearby with a shovel. This digger is neither mortal nor otherwise. For she is a robot.

Terry the robot gently shovels the top of the soil to one side. *"Are you telling me you buried Dumas and he wasn't completely dead?"* The one asking is Gee, short for the Grim Reaper. The one to answer, Lucien replies, *"He wants to be a spiritual being."* Gee's shocked, *"You gotta be kidding!"*

Lucien continues unruffled, *"If we waited until that Dumb ass was totally dead he'd be just a ghost instead of a doggy spirit."* Gee snorts, *"And who in any world gave you three permission to invent another form of spirit?... a zombie bow-wow at that?"* *"The world has just barely gotten past their notion werewolves are real.!"* Lucien, Roman and Ralph bow their heads in shame. *"This pooch ain't no werewolf sir!"* Gee looks relieved, *"He better not be!"*

Ralph in support of his cohorts mumbles, *"And just who came up with the idea of echo spirits, doggy spirits and zombies in the first place?"* *"What we're obviously doing is experimenting."* *"One time he's one thing then another."* Lucien admits *"It isn't ideal to keep changing him from one shape to another, but he seems to like it for some reason."* *"When he gets it right he will be happy,"* She pauses to think, *"I hope."*

Feeling bold, Roman adds, *"Admittedly we are in uncharted territory, but because I have a good past relationship with the dog, why don't we just assign her,* pointing to the robot *to go with this spirit and become possessed by him?"* But they've all forgotten just how smart they've allowed the robot to become. And are shocked as she stammers, *"No way Jose!"* *"Don't have fleas; don't want fleas!"* Ralph smirks, *"She picked that up from Dumb ass, I mean Dumas."* *"You have to be careful about what you say around some."*

The artificially intelligent one immediately resumes control of its' crisp proper attitude. Other angels hover above Dumas's grave discussing the dogs' dilemma. *"Gee doesn't want him to be a zombie; what is this dumb overembellished spirit dog supposed to do?"* *"What was in your mind telling him he had a choice?"*

Angela responds, *"Who ever thought he'd want to continue as a spirit after suffering the curse of aging?"* *"The spirit option was just a figure of speech... until he jumped on it."* *"Who could have guessed he even remembered when Ralph was a spirit?"* Gee just nods understandingly and sighs.

Ralph offers, *"I would be happy to follow him around."* Angela accuses, *"Still trying to be Vigilante Spirit?"* Ralph slumps in his hover, Gee points out that Angel Roman has collaborated with Dumas in the past successfully. Roman perks diplomatically, *"I do owe old*

Dumb ass a debt of gratitude for the work he did for me on two occasions."

"First he rescued Hiker from the three thieves and then from the robbers at the big house." Lucien isn't about to agree to the idea of her Ralph ever returning to his Vigilante Spirit persona. She quickly endorses Gee's plan to send Roman. She doesn't care what Roman does, as long as it doesn't involve Ralph.

Lucien exercises her authority over the others as she coyly demands, *"Roman, perhaps you can take this robot and follow Dumas temporarily."* Roman is thrilled to do anything instead of being a guardian angel to some new human again. It gets old after several millennials. *"Anything for the mission boss."* He quips. Surreptitiously Terry grits her mechanical gums. *"We will just see just who possesses whom."*

Suddenly Gee bounces up and down with the realization he's behind in his sacred duty to transport absolutely every last soul for better or worse to their ultimate destination. War, pestilence, starvation and disease are rampant throughout the world.

As usual, he doesn't bother to say *"Goodbye."* But then he decides these particular guardian angels aren't very busy. Swiftly the Grim Reaper is off collecting the deceased from everywhere. He can't allow them to just sit except in the case of the Anatomy lab. They need to be somewhere. That famous white light at the end of the terminal tunnel loses its charm and becomes scary before long.

Roman enters the robot and they take off in the direction of Dumas. Or so Roman thinks. He puts the robot on automatic in the direction of the dog spirit. Then dozes off or meditates as he will later claim. As soon as robot Terry senses his loss of control she alters course. Terry's looking for Robert, the only person human or angel she likes. Not this old angelhaulic.

Once at the government agency where Robert works, a bit too quickly she flashes her agency ID. Remembering her from when she actually worked here the guard waves her through at first.. They enter the gate of a top secret government agency. Sleeping and unaware old Roman snoozes on. Robots do what they are told to do…right? A secondary security system senses her expired pass and interior security kicks in. But the robot proceeds towards her intended objective.

Terry has tricks of her own and strides on.

Dumas is at the mountaintop cabin sees a ghost.

It's Grace's ghost. He knows she passed. For one whose soul is saved she's not happy. She's crying as she attempts over and over again to release the gate to her kennel. Her dogs are hungry. But her soul can't open the gate. Grace's body lies in repose at the chapel in the valley. Her sons and grandsons weep by her casket.

Yesterday as she reached the valley where she was to buy her locked up dogs some treats, her soul passed from this dimension. Her lovely soul was just one of those Gee was in such a hurry to transport. Now what remains up on her beloved mountaintop home can't open the gate. Dumas summons help from Roman. The sleepy angel bolts to full consciousness sensing the robot he thought he possessed hugging Robert instead. He screams at her, *"Get your hot rivets the hell out of here!"* Robert who is speaking with Terry is shocked…literally. His teeth rattle so hard the guards are alerted. Terry the robot he robot has him in a lip lock and just won't let go.

Dumas approaches Grace who doesn't recognize him at first. She turns and implores him not to hurt her poor animals. He settles peacefully and calms her. *"Perhaps if we work on the kennel gate together we can release them." "Would you like to work together?"* She relaxes noticeably but quickly her aura hardens. *"I know you!"*

"You were once my sons' retriever." He smiles. *"Observe carefully." "My mother was a retriever; my old man was a mastiff."* "A very small part of me is retriever." Now Grace is furious. *"You're the very one who bit both of my sons!" "Why should I trust you?"* He sniffs, *"Please consider it my penance for past misdeeds madam." "My intentions are entirely honorable."*

Poor Grace has never been called *"madam"* during her lifetime and it strikes her as a ridiculous remark. *"My dogs are starving!" "I guess I have no choice."* Dumas spirit ignores her anger because he knows she can't shoot him. *"Ok, let's try to open it together."*

There aren't padlocks. The only thing holding the gate in place is the wooden peg she stuck in the lock hole. A mighty shove by both using all of their combined strength pops them from their hasps. Her dogs are out; the hounds are on the loose. Bears make themselves scarce, bobcats scat. For hungry hounds are a hunting.

Like most familiar with the wilderness her hounds will have an easy time finding something. Grace fades in an upward flow as her ghost chases her beautiful soul. All who live on the mountain are sad. Dumas heads in another direction to wherever. Grace has gone to heaven and her dogs are out. He has done his job without Roman and the robot.

Choosing to find adventure, North is his new direction, wherever that takes him. Ignoring big cities he then passes into farmlands nearly lost in time. Below is Pennsylvania Amish country.

He's over a square farm with four equal roads sporting two barking dogs. He's just above them.

Dumas floats just overhead, like a balloon but neither looks up. They sense something is near. It's their job to protect this farm and so they run in an endless charge around four corners. Dumas tries to calm them, They only run faster until they drop in exhaustion. Dumas feels sorry for them but doesn't stop. Something more urgent lies just beyond the trees. It's a mother dog with her litter.

"A careless moment with a worthless hound and here I am stuck with four curs." They didn't have the daddy they were supposed to have. Still she feels a mothers' love and they nurse without any sense of their impending doom should they be found out. They have little value to this farm. Dumas knows he's also a mongrel and feels sorry for them.

Dumas looks with pity upon this sad bunch and sets out to find some loving children in a nearby town. Some who aren't concerned with an American Kennel club pedigree. These children's guardian angels will line up to relieve the mama dog when the time is right for them to be weaned. The sooner the better.

Eventually momma dog is going to wean them find her way back to the farmhouse, The home where she belongs. No one will give a second thought to where she's been. As for her, she's wiser for wear. In the future she won't fall for the doubtful charms of a traveling hound dog. But it's hard to fool the Amish when it comes to animals.

They understand and don't scold her for her folly. No one, including mama dog says a word when she's locked in her kennel as her season comes again. As the farmer puts it, *"No market for curs."* And *"Everything and everyone here has to earn its' own way."*

3

Gone to the dogs

Once upon a time, more human children were born than there were guardian angels. Too many new little new souls to assign on a one-to-one basis. Now there are more than enough angels. For the human desire to have guardians has diminished. Although many are born many aren't presented.

Our canine friends aren't eligible for these celestial beings. Just the same canines are constantly evolving and increasing. New breeds of puppies show up each year. Even with programs to spay and neuter.

Ralph wonders, *"When the last human passes from the earth, will dogs takeover?"* Lucien reads his mind and answers. *"No, their lives are too short, and they would need hands instead of paws to run things."* *"Sentient robots will probably destroy mankind and take over this world at the rate they are progressing."* *"Remember Ralph we exist to serve."*

Ralph says, *"Dog gone, that means we're getting new babies to watch over instead of the puppy I want."* Lucien smirks, *"This is the last time you pull that nonsense on me."* He laughs at her, *"Wanna bet?"* *"You're easy"* Although nothing is said of it now, all three are determined to prevent earths' takeover by self-aware heartless robots.

As for their dog, if the truth is told, Dumas is fierce, ugly and never smelled very good. Even so he found a family who loved him when he was young. In truth no one really loves him now that he's old. His mostly buried corpse doesn't improve the quality of his ambiance. Angels smell only what they choose. Stinky Dumas isn't their choice scent. So, they don't choose to smell anything like Dumas.

Without admitting anything to each other, angels Ralph and Lucien go in opposite directions with the idea of looking after their dog. Lucien loves Ralph so she tolerates Dumas. Any criticism from the Grim Reaper stings. Lucien has enough of this duality of Dumas for now. She touched a spot of fur sticking through the dirt in which his body rests. He awakened looking ten years younger than when he was buried.

Ralph moans, *"Lucy, This isn't what I meant by a puppy!"* *"I realize you are trying to restore the natural order."* *"However, one manifestation of this dog is still a spirit; the other is mortal."* She replies, *"It isn't the first time"* *"Remember when I pretended to be someone else...when I convinced you to propose to me?"* Ralph is speechless and tries to think about something else. He can't. Dumas is back together in just one piece...for now.

Strange lights that just aren't right!...

In an entirely different paradigm, Sergeant Mark is discussing mysterious lights reported at the technical school with his captain. *"It seems the school has closed its' doors for good with a half dozen projects just sitting unfinished on a long workbench." "The school is bankrupt."*

The captain replies, *"That is horrible." "Those kids have the brightest young minds this side of MIT." "I wouldn't be surprised if some of them don't try to get in to retrieve their projects." "And I wouldn't blame them, but of course we can't condone such activities."*

"Tell you what Mark, Keep an eye on the place and tell the others too also, but as long as there's no visible signs of vandalism or destruction, just leave it alone... for now." "Ok with you?" Mark agrees, *"And of course we didn't have this conversation."* Mark shrugs, *"What conversation?"* His lapel recorder is completely in the off mode.

On another side of the great forest...

Dumas having been recombined, manages to remain just out of sight. Having put Terry the robot into a higher gear than she knew she has, to pick up litter, Roman is quite comfortable. The better side of this old angel returns.

Once he regained his pleasant nature after staying sober with the help of his angel alcoholics anonymous chapter. Before that he was a mess especially around beer bubbles. Since becoming stone cold sober, Roman has even stopped sniffing honey suckle. He and the robot slow down and circle and try to find and follow Dumas at a distance. Chasing one's tail isn't that unusual among the sneaky. Terry mutters to herself, *"He ain't nowhere nohow."*
Lucien leave Ralph to his buddies and is working with others who have tails…

Lucien checks in on the adoption process of the Amish puppies sent to town. Just one finds its' way to Lucien, or vice versa. At first she didn't care much about Dumas because he was grown up when they came together. But she finds this puppy irresistible.

Hugging the puppy as best an angel can, Lucien asks the baby compliant puppy. *"What does my little doggy want to eat?"* The doggy doesn't respond to her but stares directly into her eyes with a hypnotic gaze. Lucien realizes the puppy has been possessed by a demon. She pretends to be under its' spell.

The demon demands, *"Show me where to find the ghost of Will Gold."* Lucien responds in a faint weak tone. *"I don't have any gold."* The demon insists. She calls Ralph to show him how to slaughter demons, but he doesn't answer. He's off on his own quest. To follow Roman and the robot, who are following no one. Dumas is now following Roman. No one told him about the mortal and spirit dog reuniting. Raven was following Dumas too. She's figured it all out.

Back to Lucien and the demonic puppy, again, the demon growls at her, *"Take me to William Gold."* Submissively the physical manifestation of Lucien thumps

47

the puppy on its' head. *"Follow me."* Nonplussed over the ringing in its' ears the demonic canine runs to catch up with his supposed hypnotic subject, thinking *"This just isn't supposed to happen!"* They approach the haunt of the late William Gold. It's just below the span of the old viaduct.

Demon dog is worried, *"This was supposed to be really easy."* William Gold ignores his impending transfer into the pits of hell. Demonic puppy approaches wagging his tail furiously and squeaks, *"Get on your feet loser."* *"You have an appointment with my master in the next 10 minutes."* William Gold moves as directed with his imaginary feet.

In an apparent hypnotic trance, Lucien and Gold are led to a familiar spot in the river. A hole where hell meets the world of sunshine. The three stand quietly as the demon summons his master the devil. As hellhole opens in the river the waters boil and immediately become red steam. Lucien dispossesses the puppy's demon; the devil roars, *"Whose stupid idea was it to think they could temp this angel?"*

"This is insane." A whiney voice replies from the inferno, *"Yours sir!"* Dumas thinks to himself, *"And they called me Dumb ass before I was Dumas." "The devils as dumb as hell."* The devils forgets Dumas is partly spirit and sarcastically yells, *"Bite me!"* And Dumas quickly does just that.

Overcoming the rage emanating from hell, a loud roar is heard coming further downstream. No longer is the Grim Reaper hampered by the slow elegant sailing ship the *El Muerte*. The ship is replaced by The *El Muerte II,* the fastest most powerful muscle ship ever. The vortex created sucks the steam from the air creating a scarlet cushion for Gee's vessel. He plows past both Lucien and Will Gold driving the demon directly down into the abyss of hell.

A scream is heard from Satan as the door to hell slams on him crushing both demon and master back to hell like trash into a rusty compactor. The miracle of it all is the river. It's silted in here to a depth of only one foot. It's very deep though within the dimension of devils and angels.

A faithful sentry stands guard…

A grim ghost in the uniform of a Civil War soldier mopes sullenly. As they pass it shouts *"Halt, who goes there?"* No answer. *"Who goes there?"* Still no answer. He raises his rifle and fires. But hits nothing. Amused, Lucien thinks to herself, *"And that is why you're still here."* The soldier grumbles something and spits his tobacco chaw in their direction.

"On your feet Corporal." Gee commands the ghost of the Union soldier. He doesn't budge.

"What is your problem?" *"Your duty was over almost 200 years ago."* The soldier still will not budge.

Gee asks the soldier why he won't accompany him to a better place. The ancient soldier boy tells the angel of death, *"I received a direct order not to leave this bridge until I have kept it from being destroyed by a Confederate saboteur or when relieved by another. or when hell freezes over whichever comes first."* Lucien thinks she has a solution.

Seconds later, the very overdue Confederate soldier in grey mounted upon a great black stallion brandishing a rusty saber gallops up to them and swings his mighty blade. Not at his Union adversary but directly at the huge viaduct. A small chunk is chopped off falling into the river below. It flows again with pent up power carrying the rocks out of sight. The faithful boy soldier fires.

The saboteur is vanquished into the wind. Moments later a Union Army officer arrives to dismiss the lad. The faithful young soldier states *"I am relieved and very ready to go."* His weapon vanishes in the breeze. And the mighty *El Muerte II* has its next passenger. He's astonished to be greeted with a handshake by the Confederate cavalryman he thinks he's just shot. *"I was assigned the job of attacking the viaduct back in 1861."* "It would have helped if you rode just a little bit faster," his new best friend replies.

Gee guides the *El Muerte II* to its celestial destination. More goodbyes as they ascend. Lucien states the obvious," *At least Gee wasn't complaining."* Along with several friendly ghosts they flow up the hill very satisfied with their work. The ghosts hang around for a while. Then sensing they were wearing out their welcome they fly off in the direction of Annapolis where all of the great old haunts remain. Occasionally even old George Washington's ghost shows up. Once he had the teeth he was born with again he couldn't stop smiling until he saw his reflection.

Dumas is back at the big house where he lived so happily. He peers over his own grave. Looking down at the place where his body recently lay he feels something. Growls, *"I have no desire to lay back down."* Once again when he's asked whether he wants to rest with his body beneath the earth he reaffirms his desire to remain a spiritual being. Lucien just sighs and thinks, *"Once a dumb ass…"* Dumas worries, that with all of his shapes shifting he might meet himself in the flesh coming back.

Pretending to be thinking it over to appease Lucien, he dog spirit lays momentarily upon this familiar hollow. For the first time since he died Dumas feels well and together. But it isn't true; he isn't quite together. And he isn't quite sure how to deal with being young again.

This past day was the most interesting one since long ago when his spirit expelled the evil spirits stalking Grace's home. Dumas doesn't know it now, but with her passing that service won't be needed again. He's worried he's run out of things to do as a spirit. A very confused old owl just stares and wonders.

Temptation snakes its way again….

The devil whispers up the pipe to old Will Gold. *"We can use another tarnished soul." "You've been sitting by this old bridge for a long time." "No one has offered you a ride upstairs in all that time." "And they won't, will they?"* Will just listens and doesn't respond to Satan.

"Why do you think that is?" Will stammers. *"Because the only things I gave up to others were things I couldn't use." The devil sneers to let this retched souls own words sink in." "So, you only were charitable to gain what?"   "A   tax   deduction   at   best?"*

"When would I have filed for a charitable deduction...after I was dead?" Will denies filed a tax return after he transferred billions to his daughter as he was plunging to his death over a dam. He realizes the devil doesn't really know him and is trying to tempt, as he always does. The devil counters. *"You only gave AFTER you couldn't use the money." "It wasn't charity; it was a silly attempt to save your soul!" "You are damned!"* Will replies, *"If what you're saying is true, why am I up here and you are down there?"*

Will Gold confesses, *"I was wrong not to have cared for my daughter before dying."* *"May the good Lord please forgive me!"* Upon hearing his sincere confession and plea to the Lord his arch enemy, Satan gags in anger. Then retreats the rest of the way down into the portal of hell. Dumas howls with joy. A chorus of nearby ghosts chant *"The devil be damned!"*

Gee tells Will *"Do you realize you have managed to shut off your access to both heaven and hell with just one set of words."* *"What did you hope to accomplish by a plea to God?"* People can pray for the dead, but not the dead for the dead.

Will doesn't answer for a moment. Then tells this ominous angel of death, *"Honesty with myself is balm to my soul."* He echoes the chant, *"The devil be damned!"*

From nearby, Dumas is very confused, *"I don't understand."* *" I guess it's why the angels call me Dumb ass."* Will flows back to his ledge at the edge of the wall where he just may stay forever. Nevertheless forever for Will isn't going to take very much longer. Because One who matters the most was listening.

As soon as these angels and ghosts are over the hill and out of sight and can't easily hear, Gee turns to a hidden apparition. *"Well what do you have to report?"* His voice is highly enthusiastic as he gives Gee a full report on Will Gold. *"Mr. Gold has been an exemplary individual since passing."* *"Conceding the obvious, his living years were as an uncut gem"*

"The living man was buried behind his wealth and was hidden from reality." *"It was a fools' paradise."* *"He wanted to be cool but didn't realize the serious nature of his folly."* It's a troublesome problem with the immature and foolish of all weak mortal flesh.

"But when he started with nothing, he nurtured others as the persona of Spirit with admirable grace and compassion for both man and beast." *"His essence was*

realized when Spirit merged with another latent saint."
"As you know she had lain dormant nearly in a state of
purgatory as well." "They were exemplary as the being we
know as Vigilante Spirit as you yourself used him several
times." Gee listens, says nothing but knows these words are
true.

"And as it is completely possible to allow their
offspring our good guardian angel Ralph to remain a
separate being and husband to Lucien it is my opinion that
Will Gold be elevated post haste." "As we both know the
other team has made him a tempting offer, which to Will's
credit he turned down." Gee is sorry to lose such a valuable
spy stationed by the porthole to hell on the Patapsco. He
just acknowledges, *"He's earned his mansion in the sky."*

Quickly he spins his great ship around and before
Will Gold's ghost is swept up into *El Muerte II*, Will's
ghostly sheet is released and flying down the river. With it
gone, only a dignified fig leaf covers his imaginary

57

personal parts as St. Peter waives them through the pearly gates of heaven.

This affair isn't without incident as St. Peter writes out a moving citation for Gee. It states **Excess Speeding through the Pearly Gates.** He will later point out *"While it's bad enough to lose the passengers' white sheet, it is quite another to grab onto old St. Pete's toga."*

On the human side…

The Howard County news media reports-

Patapsco River reverses flow for an hour

A river reversing its' course is just a curiosity to any normal person. Because some do, but not this one. Scientists come and perform whatever tests they can imagine. They take water samples and ultimately release their opinion. It was just an illusion; it really didn't happen.. Everyone decides it is just another fluke…like UFO's once were.

However, world events eclipse it shortly and public attention drifts to more explainable things.

Sergeant Mark knows something weird saved his life. He can't imagine what it was and decides to chalk it off as something he'll never know. He knows he didn't turn on the camera that saved his life, job and cost him a faithless wife. He read the item about the river and so he decides to go fishing on his day off. *"Maybe this IS something I can figure out."*

With his bait can of worms and a cheap rod and reel he sets off to the Patapsco. It's warm but the ground is still too damp to sit on. Casting out to the center of the river he peels out the line so he can sit on the bench. It is the same bench at the bottom of the big house on the hill where a demon was once lured a demon to its doom. One where Dumas now protects a fool perched at a porthole to hell.

Dumas isn't feeling as energetic today as he has been. Even as his recombined body is younger than it was before he died, today just isn't the same. He feels his spirit sagging a bit as he watches the man he saved from being shot. Just jousting with demons at each cast of his fishing line.

And the demon patiently waits for the line to land in the portal. But it doesn't. Because his old retriever sense actually enjoys playing fetch at each cast of the line. Finally Ralph shows up and whispers to this poor fool," *Don't keep tempting fate!"*

When Spirit Dumas reunited with his dead dog self, something good rubbed off. Some of his fleas are giving him a second chance. That itch stirs up so much vitality in the dog he cheer up to living by another few percent. But his fleas aren't happy. One cries, *"He's stale!"*

Spirit dog Dumas is interested in getting even with every creature who desecrated his grave. Including the owl, pussycats, polecats and even the new puppy who now occupies his favorite place on the porch. A demonic urge to get even overcomes him. He struggles yet can barely move. He thinks, *"Maybe tomorrow."* And settles back to sleep. All of is old fleas except for the haughty one jump for joy, *"He's back!"*

Then word comes down through the mystical chain of command the idea of dog spirits is out of the question. Just that. No instructions. No orders. The spirit is gradually absorbed back into the worse for wear Dumas. He scratches until he finds himself staring into the back barrel of the puppy who replaced him. A sharp snap of his gritty teeth on the tail of his desecrater sends the offending furball yelping down the road in search of a dog catcher. And never to return. Said dog warden will later claim, *"It's the first time I ever had one roll into the truck hunched up like it just saw a ghost."* Which in fact it did.

With Dumas up and in one piece again the problem for the angels becomes obvious. This dog isn't really same age as when he was buried. It's much younger. For one thing the side facing down didn't have any fur left on it. Dumas was one half bald faced. Puppy essence trickling down on him over several weeks had really sunk in. His other side was still intact; it was weird. Any polecats in the area would find his scent overbearing,

Even reconstructed, he couldn't catch any because they would smell poor Dumas way too soon. But one duck hunter does accidently manage to feed him as he dropped his bird and runs for his life. Having vanquished his competition at the big house on the hill Dumas trots down to the river to get a drink. It's the same duck hunter whose catch Dumas stole once before. It happens just after he sees Dumas smile and catches a whiff of his scent. He whines to his wife, *"I'm going to start hunting over on the Eastern Shore." "This place is too weird."*

Over on Maryland's *"SHORE"* as it's referred to by locals, an informal good spirit meeting is held at a venerable Ocean City hotel bar. After several rounds of cheer the straw poll issued the statement, *"All good dogs go to heaven. "Who would want to go to heaven if no dogs are there!"*

4

Shaggy dog

Dumas takes stock of himself. His spirit self has subsided. He's really ticked off about heaven. Perhaps if he knew a small survey on St. Valentines' Day of 2022, asked about a dogs' chances to go to heaven, and they conclude dogs should. He might have hope and what follows might not have. As in the case of his human counterparts no one advised his of his saintly potential. A very wise angel tries to warn, *"Demons always await despair."* Unheard by Dumas, this warning is just noise in the wind.

Roman is shocked to realize that his idea of following Dumas is derailed. Terry who he trusted to be on automatic *follow Dumas* autopilot is getting the bums rush from a government agency building due to her expired credentials. Her escorts are polite but firm. The reason she's not arrested is the old Director is back to running the agency. Only he and a few others know Terry is a robot because they've rented her and her associates from Lorenzo in the past. He will call Lorenzo over when he gets home and explain, *"We just can't have these creatures coming and going whenever they want."* Lorenzo will nod and agree in bewilderment.

His conveyance had a mind to visit her beloved Robert. They are exiting the building under armed escort. The old angel waits until they are in the car borrowed back at the house to resume control.

She is loopy but determined to resume her quest at some later time. Trying to beat him to the punch as he fumes, she asks in a giddy tone, *"If I didn't update my agency pass is so bad, what about your driver's license?"*

He just replies, *"Turn left at the next roundabout."* She smirks but knows that angels don't need licenses. *"Where is YOUR driver's license?"*

He won't play her game. *"You are one sarcastic bucket of bolts, aren't* you?*"* Terry replies in an annoying machine voice. *"Glove compartment!"* Roman finally realizes. This machine has become way too smart. He reaches in and pulls out her license, registration and current insurance card. Roman is impressed.

At this moment, his leader Lucien and husband Ralph are on their own ruse.

Angels Lucien and husband Ralph are trying not to cross paths with the Grim Reaper. Gee thinks they have actually gone to the dogs. They're visiting an angel named Mike at the Anatomy lab at a university in Baltimore. After a rough start they're now good friends.

When Ralph and Lucien met, Mike was one the first angels they met as a couple. But only after a brawl between

Mike and Ralph, before he became an angel, that nearly shut down the inner city. It was an adventure the friends did not reminisce about. It was the day Mike and Ralph tried to have a fight in the middle of the street next to the hospital. It stopped traffic.

Angel feathers were all over the place. Lucien intervened in a pitched battle that left feathers, dust and tender feelings. At one point she threatened to wake up all of the cadavers. It was a mess before peace. Since then the two groups of angels have cooperated in many escapades.

Mike and the other Anatomy Lab angels faithfully guard the earthly remains of kind people who donated their bodies for the advancement of science. Hopefully, Gee will see an angelic reason for their trip. After remembering some but not all of their adventures Ralph and Lucien return to the big house.

No one misses the puppy or Dumas at the big house because nowadays the Lorenzo family no longer cares much about reality. There's a virtual world cloaked around them now. And his business of course. The robots were glad to see the dogs gone. Because they always managed to find the slippery spots on the lawn. Way too often. The fog rolls down the Patapsco and recombined Dumas rolls on. And thinks that he may never die again. He's almost right.

With all of the people who recently passed waiting for transport, the grim reaper is too busy to look for the angels to give them the word. *"Dumas must live or die but not both at the same time." "For that's the domain of demons."*

So the reblended Dumas falls through the cracks for now. He has a sense of pride though. When he reaches a clean pond he thoroughly bathes off the dirt from his temporary grave and the other indignities his hide endured. Although his head is still slightly lopsided, and one side looks newer than the other, he pounces with pride once again as a semi living thing. Dumas is back! He feels better than ever.

Being back doesn't mean for long. He's in an adventurous frame of mind. People have let him down and so have angels. Nothing slows his retreat from the home he's had for so long. If things aren't strange enough Dumas has just entered the neighborhood of the biggest busybody in town… Ms. Henrietta Snit.

Ms. Snit is a self-proclaimed guardian of all that is proper. Looking at mangy Dumas she takes his picture with her phone and punches 911. By sheer coincidence, the voice on the other end of the emergency center line is that of Dumas's first master. Hunter takes one look at the photo and heads out of the center.

Buzzardville's only dog catcher van is parked out front without it's driver. Keys in the truck make the job of hijacking the ominous vehicle easy. Before Dumas can make it out of sight Hunter is out of the van with a big net.

Dumas takes one look at his first master. The one who made him fetch ducks but eat polecats and decides to move first. His feet do the rest until Hunter catches up with him. The encounter doesn't turn out the way Hunter imagined it would.

Dumas has no idea how to drive anything. But his intended dog catcher is in the back wrapped in the very net he was about to use on him. Henrietta Snit swoons after witnessing the event. Dumas stops her from hurting herself but can't leave any witnesses behind. Soon Henrietta and Hunter find themselves sharing the same crate.

Both are very circumspect. When one breathes in the other breathes out. It's uncomfortable but no one's hurt. Dumas is oblivious to their plight and proceeds with his flight from thankless humans and their angels. A ghost is shocked. *"The dude's breaking bad!"*

Hunter and the lady are so tangled in the cramped cage they find themselves in a more intimate situation than either innocent has ever encountered. Hunter breaks their embarrassment by stating, *"I know that dog, he has a history of biting!"*

Clinging to Hunter in exaggerated fright, Henrietta just sighs, *"Are you married?"* He answers, *"Yes, you?"* She just groans, *"What a way to meet a guy!"* And she pretends to be trying to unravel the tangles in the net the dog snarled them in. Then she queries, *"Are you still with your wife or anyone else?"*

Fearing she'll leave him bound up forever he lies, *"No "* A nosy ghost murmurs *"Is that your nose Pinocchio! "* She thinks some and asks, *"Why did you come to get the dog?"* He answers, *"That was my dog; the dumb ass ran away!"* She says, *"Was he a really good one?"*

Hunter replies, *"He was the worst dog anyone ever had!"* She thinks some more and asks, *"Then why did you take the dog van you aren't supposed to drive and come all of this way?" "Was it my beauty; did you wish to meet me?"*

He snorts, *"NO!"* thinking the dog has more appeal than you. *"Then why?"* she demands. He lies, *"I just wanted to drive the doggy van." "I always wanted to."* Dumas can't stand to listen to one more word of this people poop. He pulls up under a shaded tree and pops out.

Dumas's strength has come back, and he is running like the wind. But his eyes still look like those of a zombie. The big dog slows down as he reaches a doggy park where a half dozen others are playing and doing doggie things under the watchful eyes of their owners.

One kind doggy person sees him as a rescue. Then slips a collar around his neck and has the new rescue fed, bathed, shaved and vaccinated. Dumas has a new home if he wants one. But after all of this loving care he slips away once more. Dumas thinks, *"I didn't need a home; I just needed a real bath." "My fur is so knotted; I feel like the worlds' worst shaggy dog."*

5

The Pack

A new day is upon Dumas and hopefully a better one. His aging carcass feels better now than it was when he was young. And he has strange new qualities that carried over from his time as a spirit. Who is responsible? Neither heaven nor hell is willing to accept blame. No demon is interested in this abomination.

Roman, the angel who started Dumas on his odyssey of dog spirit is assigned to keep him safe. More importantly, to keep Dumas from further screwing up the natural order of the world. As the subject of this dilemma, Dumas doesn't know much of heaven or hell. He just wants to explore. His outlook is good. But his hybrid dog-spirit state is really an impossible one to maintain.

Poor Dumas hasn't a clue about what led him to alert the lawman his wife was about to shoot him. In reality his weird powers are a residual element of all that came before. It started when a well-meaning spirit enhanced his intelligence.

His ferocity was unleashed when Roman transformed him into a fierce beast with the strength to save a victim from being killed. It was Hiker, his last master a robbery victim. Another time when it served their purposes the angels borrowed his spirit to defeat demons threatening Grace.

Each time an increasing residue of something not within his normal instinctive mind remained within; Although he seemingly returned to his normal state,. Now, none who utilized Dumas truly know him. Only Roman is still around. This angel just observes what he considers the saga of Dumbass and wonders, *"What next?"* Mortals are doing the same with sentient robots.

Roman finds who he sometimes refers to as Dumb ass peacefully asleep in the burned out ruins of the old cabin from which he once fled. His head rests upon the very spot where he once lay down when he was allowed in.

His old fleas are having a discussion involving the pros and cons of invading the unnatural hide of this crazy animal. The nays have it and they pass Roman without giving a damn about his status as a potential celestial. Maybe there will be a fox or even a coyote in the nearby church graveyard. *"We the fleas do as we please."* While furious at their insolence, angels just don't talk to fleas.

The church graveyard is as always a center of gossip. Few folks are coming, many going. When the dogs' familiar silhouette appears no one is alarmed. He's been here many times before. And he's a nice dog. Not like the ones who lift their leg at every stone. A deaf old deacon inquires, *"What's his real name?"* A chorus rings out *"Dumb ass!"* Dumas is insulted.

No manicured green turf surrounds them. Not a highly polished granite reflects the light.
All the ground is covered with stones and moss. And not enough of the moss. It's a down to dirt respite. Yet Dumas is here for a reason and won't be distracted.

He sits raising his paw. *"Was Mark the missing twin?"* A polite voice responds, *"Whose child is missing?"* These folks have no answers. And the souls all know Dumas knows they don't know. An old grouch grumbles, *"No wonder the angels call you Dumb ass!"*

A naughty hind leg lifts with a mind of its' own then drenches that respite to mud. A deacon spouts, *"He isn't nice anymore."* Dumas retorts. *"Isn't there a Darwinist in here somewhere?" "I think I hear monkeys."* Another tries to throw a stone to chase him. Then grabs his own chest. Too late he realizes he can't have another heart attack; he's deceased already.

Hating being called names, he, trots away from the graveyard as quickly as his clean shaven, sweet, groomed body can carry his semi athletic dog body. Like once before he plunges into the great forest in a new direction, it's one he's never been.

Suddenly Dumas stops frozen inn his tracks. His nose points up. A scent of danger. He's stumbled into a group of strays. It's one led by an alpha male. It's mostly the males' half grown pups and one female. This cold fierce predator suffers no other male in his domain. One he alone determines to be his own. Before Dumas can offer apologies, sniff noses or other parts the leader attacks grabbing at this intruders' throat. One brief moment this death grip holds then slips. And it would have been over except for something unseen.

This unseen is within the victim as Dumas anticipates the attack. He has his aggressors' demise staged in just two defensive steps. *"He grabs, I parr, I reverse it; his windpipe is crushed." "It's just that simple, click, click, click."*

Dumas awaits his attacker in poised readiness. Only the faintest disconcerting smile sits upon his furry lips. Then something overhead freezes him. He's rendered numb. His attacker leaps clamping his fangs on Dumas. Wham! As if this pooch is punched, his eyes roll up like shades. And he falls dead in a heap. Dumas and the pack are astonished. Even more so as he realizes he knows one other here from a long time ago. *"It's Princess!"*

The leader of the pack is dead; long live the new leader.

He's happened upon a lady dog who once before he knew. This old friend has an inquisitive pup. It was from a litter of four. Although he was the last of the litter born, is the first to notice Dumas. It complains, *"Mama who is that ugly dog?"* His mama replies, *"He might be your papa."* He's insistent, *"Mama, is that my papa?"* She demurs. *"Could be." "You're ugly the same way."*

Her sarcasm is a ruse; he's big strong and somehow stronger than he was when last they met. As she follows her paws become raw, yet he plods ever onwards mile after mile. Up hills down into valleys. His paws barely touch the ground. It seems as though Dumas is walking on air. Finally they rest for the night. The season is changing. It's colder and colder.

The puppy doesn't care as he thinks, *"I just don't give a dog damn." "Everybody needs to be somewhere."* And snuggles closer snuggling to his momma for warmth.

The night is cold, and the wind is blowing a light snow across the mountain. And not an angel cares. Dumas thinks, *" At least not unless someday if dogs replace people."* *"Then they will."*

The puppy asks if Dumas is his dad. His mother lies and says Dumas is his father. *"I would remember such a thing!"* Not that he's never wandered astray. But not with this lying witch. He starts to tell the truth to the pup but is stopped by Roman who has heard everything.

"Say you're his dad." "He doesn't understand the biology of the creatures he possesses." "He might be a better dog if he thinks he should be like you." Dumas is way out of his league. *"I'm your daddy dawgg!"* Dumas has never had puppies with anyone. He's mostly been alone with people and angels.

The angel Roman explains to Dumas why he wasn't allowed to defend himself against the old pack leader. He warns *"Once you kill one of your own kind the path to repetition is set." "You have too much strength for the mystical world to allow you to deal with killing and death."* Dumas growls affirmation.

Dumas reluctantly follows Roman's direction; The pack is to turn the puppies in at the Buzzardville shelter. They go as they have been directed by Dumas.. For now Dumas is the new leader of the pack and the puppies have been sent to the pound. The rest of the pack leaves as well. The pup who thinks Dumas is his dad is picked to lead them back. Princess tells him to be a good boy, licks away his tears, and kisses him goodbye.

Princess sees the Dumas she once met when her eyes were bright and young. That Dumas shared his duck and she the chicken she lifted in Buzzardville. Now her head is heavy, and her tail dangles low. For time and litters of puppies have had its' way with her. She can't keep up the pace.

As for her sense of Dumas, in her reality she knows he cannot be the same dog. And he doesn't help. Moreover he has a strange grin. Dogs may grin but not like this. This hotdog smiles more like the dogcatcher she once dodged than a canine.

It's clear she is welcome to stay with him. She will as long as he catches something to eat which he hasn't so far. Her offspring are weaned and gone. *" I'm an empty nester now and free as a bird."* And thinking of that the hungrier she gets. .

And as always, Dumas trots on without a care until Roman inspires him. Dumas turns toward his first and only feminine interest. Roman is satisfied he's giving good direction to his best dog. *"Keep Princess in your sights."* Roman hasn't consumed anything to drink since joining Angels Anonymous. And dog spirits have no need for food. Dumas was never a beer bubble sniffer to the extent both Roman and Ralph were.

Roman has been unfortunate in his own personal relationships area. His first love, Lucien, married Ralph. His ability to relate to others was badly interrupted by his angel-alcoholism. Sniffing beer bubbles to be exact.

He is gradually overcoming his problem but is wary of substance temptations. Especially beer bubbles. Back in his worst times he failed to fulfill his mystical duties as a guardian angel. And he was called out publicly on more than one occasion by not only his peers but even lesser spirits.

He tries to keep his act together and is warily thinking of dating another member of his angel substance group. Roman has his own love interest. Her name is *Willow*. It's risky but they are both very determined to hover and flow straight. Having set Dumas in the right direction and having no immediate human charge he lets' her know he's flying by whenever possible. Love between any two celestials is quite boring and spiritual by earthly standards.

He doesn't know Willow's true angel name. In their group that's the way it is. So Willow doesn't know his either. Willow is a nice name. It is only their sympatico that matters. He draws near to where she attends to the human infant she is charged with watching over.

Her mind smiles and his is bathed by its' aura. *"How is the little one today?"* She whispers. *"Trying to drive us all crazy!"* It's been awhile since Roman has been through the teething stage of development with one of his charges. But he remembers not quite fondly.

"I hope to earn the Lord's confidence enough to suffer like this again." "I see you have, and I'm proud of how far you have come since we met." Willow smiles at him and again he is happy. *"There are more than enough angels now." "It doesn't reflect upon you."*

"People would rather pretend than be real." *"Perhaps it is the end of their era."* *"Dogs are prospering though."* *"Maybe your friend Dumas is just a pilot project?"* *"Willow my love, Dumas and this child you watch over may just be a pilot project for you and me!"* Her smile changes to an almost girlish giggle. *"You think?"* *As she reads his mind reflecting, "I hope not!"* They both laugh out loud.

Dumas and his new pack of one hear and pause. They stops to sniff the breeze. She wonders, *"Something to eat?"* She turns and looks back to Dumas. Nothing!. He is the same old pup she once knew but on one horrible diet. They sniff and head off together down the trail.

They're on an adventure...together. Her puppies are gone.

Her offspring appear at just the right time to become pets for the children. The fancy puppies from the breeders for sale in pet stores come with AKC pedigrees and are priced accordingly. These from Princess are free.

Their price is just great for this small town. Not everyone needs a pedigreed pup. Because this is just old Buzzardville.

Buzzardville, however, isn't an altogether happy place. Although its' late in the morning and she should be in her office, the sheriff is still relaxing in her warm tub. The reality of her job sets in when she hears banging on her front door. Loud and hard enough to awaken the dead. Leaping from the tub, she grabs the big bath towel from a hook on the door and races to answer whoever needs the sheriff. She remembers she might need her weapon.

Grabbing her service weapon from the table while gripping the towel she cracks open the door. The dog catcher sees more of her than intended as she points the pistol upward while peeping as the door swings wide open. As he comes into view, the towel comes up and the gun goes down.

This poor bug-eyed public servant cannot unsee what was seen. He blurts, *"Dogs are everywhere!"* *"They've kidnapped 911!"* The sheriff stands dripping in the doorway insanely trying to decide whether to just shoot this fool to save her own embarrassment.

As she closes the door she tells her dog catcher she's going to contact the FBI. But she won't because- *"What happens in Buzzardville stays in Buzzardville."* Dropping everything, she climbs back in the tub to think it over the idea, *"The town's gone to the dogs a long time ago."*

She finds the dog catcher at the bakery and greets him wearing her clothes and gun in holster sipping his coffee. He is calmer now with her to protect him from the pack of curs that followed him. *"Now why do you think they kidnapped him?"* It all seems more logical now that Hunter has stolen the dog van now but so absurd to think the dogs could drive. So, the two haul out the big reserve of dog kibbles and the hungry pack follows them into a fenced enclosure.

Water to wash down the dry dog food is much appreciated by the pack. Seeing they are on the verge of all trying to lick them the two public servants make their way out locking the gate and the pack of yelping pups behind. A small posse is rounded up. Consisting of the barber and two cosmetologists, they fan out in all directions. The two dog van captives await rescue happily. They decided they like one another.

The sheriff confides to the dog catcher she's always had a crush on him. And that in her culture any man who sees a lady the way he saw her this morning must marry her within a day.

"Do you understand what you need to do?" she asks. *"Yes ma'am I do."* *"I GOTTA GET OUTA TOWN FAST!"* Returning home to another warm tub she hums, *"And another one bites the dust!"*

Meanwhile, Dumas and starving Princess plod up and down a long mountain trail hours away from the place far from where they renewed their friendship…and she became widowed.

Approaching an overlook, they are overtaken by a flock of mischief makers who fly around them heckling and pecking. These are plain crows and seem to bet nothing special except their numbers.

"Who said you could come up here?" The self-appointed inquisitor makes threatening thrusts at Dumas who parries with a toothy smile. This is an unexpected event for no crow has ever been smiled at by such a weird creature.

The noisy flock backs off and lands at a safe distance. Princess doesn't want trouble, *"We're just passing through and will be gone in minutes."* The corby boss feels his importance has been recognized and replies,

"Well OK I guess." "Just don't mess anything up while you're here." Princess doesn't trust this crow.

Dumas smiles again creating Oh's and Ah's from the flock. And they all take flight up to the overhanging branches. Their leader rattles and orders them to attack Dumas. Each in turn dives at the poor dog. As each one touches him it crumbles. Then Dumas is surrounded by crows no mow. Roman did it again.

Finally there's only the leader now leading nothing. With a snap of his jaws Dumas experiences his first bites of this dubious delicacy. Princess jokes *"Dumas I never thought you would eat crow!"* He tosses her some crow crumbles *"It's not as filling as duck or even polecat, but it'll tide us over until we can catch something bigger."* Princess lowers her head and follows him down the mountain side with her tail tucked low but finds eating crow crumbles disgusting, thinking *"This mut is nuts!"*

She likes chicken can barely get her half of the crow down her throat. She can't stand the taste of his big favorite. Polecats and their stench nauseates her. There is no chicken here in the mountains. Finally she's had enough. *"Dumas, or Dumb ass, or whatever your name is, we need to talk."* He suspects she's angry but isn't sure.

"I miss my pups and frankly you have a crappy idea of what is good to eat." "And you're weird!" "I'm not even sure you're real." Dumas try to talk her out of wherever this conversation is going. It suddenly dawns on him that whatever they had when they first met has flown the coop.

Honestly, he can't even claim to be real. *"Now she wants   chicken!"* This final item is the deal breaker…chicken of all things! Dumas lies when he tells Princess he hates everything about chicken. He prefers duck. But with this one along, any plan to hustle anything just isn't going to work. She's too decent to swipe a fresh quacker from any hunter.

Appearing as sorry as any dumb dog can be. He wishes her good luck on her trip back to Buzzardville. And with one last good luck sniff of both ends for their very last time, Princess renounces her position as Dumas's girlfriend. It will be the last time they will ever meet. At least in this world.

He sits shivering against the rock savoring her fading scent. Wishing he isn't alone with just a recovering alcoholic angel. Dumas is so miserable that for once he isn't interested in anything whatsoever. It's weird. He didn't miss her before they got back together. He didn't enjoy her when they were just together. *"So. why do I miss her now?"* The nighttime breeze is cold. Collecting two dry sticks he saws them between his paws and a flicker of flame kindles the dry moss underneath.

But Princess isn't alone and cold. She sits by a hikers' fire, and he gives her a piece of his strip of beef jerky. And she thinks, *"Yuk!"* The fire is warm, and he lets her sleep in his tent. Dumas is alone and cold. He misses her warmth.

As the fire lights its' growing circle, he drags even more twigs with his jaws to build it higher. A spreading circle of light illuminates something a mortal dog would find alarming. A wolfpack squats on their haunches just yards away. Quietly watching and stalking him, but for what and for why? They have him outnumbered five to one. But after they saw the destruction of the crows, these who might eat Dumas, only watch. And hope for a sign of weakness; one that won't come.

Startled, he singes his whiskers. *"Eww...I know that hurts!."* *"It's one thing to eat your meat cooked; it's another to cook yourself!"* The wolves hope he cooks himself for them.

"Is that a threat?" *"No, you don't have enough meat on those old bones of yours to feed a puppy."* *"Neither did that stupid female who just left your skunky backside sitting*

at the top of our range." Dumas *glares back at the pack,* *"We go where we want." "You don't have a territory as far as I'm concerned."* Dumas bluffs. *"Anywhere I go to is my territory."*

Do you want to settle it right now?" The leader looks sheepish. *"No, we like big things with hoofs." "You have stinking taste!" "And as far as those scrawny birds you like." "There isn't enough meat on them to feed anything except you and your brainless human masters."*

"Stupid domestic animal, you smell so bad we don't even want to sniff you." The perfume from his recent bath stinks to them. The angel Roman listens and laughs. The wolf pack knows he's there. But unlike spirits, they can't see him. His laugh is enough to make the terrified pack assume a submissive stance on the ground. Dumas warns, *"One more smart remark and we will tear off your tails!"* They look away and whine.

Their leader regains his composure. "You've been wandering aimlessly and looking for something good to do." "Am I correct? Dumas relaxes and is ready to listen. *"Would you care to share the warmth of my fire?"*

The whole pack groans dissent. *"We do not consider fire as our friend."* The pack moves closer just to be polite but not closer to Dumas. *"We have been watching something down in a hollow that's from somewhere threatening to our world."* Both the dog and his angel companion are listening with interest.

"What's in it for you wolf?" The leader only shakes his head anxiously and whispers. *"Tomorrow."* Just when the first light of the new day appears from the east, they all rise as one.

Dumas follows the wolves down a faint trail, one the waning moon reveals. It's a clear path to where it's going only for any who seek it take the trouble to follow. They freeze up at an overlook. Those who look can see only the dark scrub of a species not natural. No one looks or sees. They wait for something to happen. It is about that time when something usually does.

Dumas peer down with his companions and realizes everything is contrived to camouflage the landscape. It seems unusually monochrome. A rusty iron door opens. A figure steps into the predawn gloom carrying an object strapped to its' back. It walks toward towards a place only it can discern.

A spray tank on its' back spreads dark green fluid over the area near the door. Within moments the foliage withers and is gone. The figure returns to the open door. Another emerges with a different backpack. It retraces the path of the first. He sprays a green dye over the same area as the first. It constructs a synthetic landscape. He returns several times repeatedly sculpting something. But what and why?

Dumas follows the pack back up to where they shared his campfire. Dumas stares into the leaders' eyes asking, *"I'm only a dog." "Why show me that mess?"*

The leader replies, *"Dumas you ain't no ordinary dog!"*

"I know you got an angel stashed somewhere even though I can't see him." "And you ain't no leader of a pack either." "Your lady left you after all you caught was stupid crows." "You and that poor old female dog hadn't stopped to get a drink of water in the last three days." "There's something seriously unusual about you."

"Between you and whatever you got with you; the problem down below is your problem now." "Please don't follow us." "We are getting gone." "Adios!" And with that the pack exits the campfire and runs down another hidden trail.

6

A down to dirt talk

Roman looks at Dumas; Dumas looks at Roman. Neither speaks. But a whole lot of common sense is about to come forth. Roman begins with: *"Dumas..."* Dumas is relieved he's not being addressed as Dumb ass. So it's a friendly start. *"Let us enumerate some of the other reasons why you are no longer the dog that once trotted up to the big house where you lived." "OK?"*

"Just as the wolf said, you haven't eaten anything other than one-half of that crow for days." "The only girl you ever liked left you and you don't care." "An entire pack of wolves who could have eaten you in 10 minutes and although they were hungry, humbly deferred to you." "You

suddenly returned to your youthful state." "Doesn't any of this seem strange to you?" Dumas just looks puzzled. *"Doesn't it occur to you that you aren't really alive?"* Dumas doesn't reply but the realization he's no longer himself sinks in.

Dumas scoots back to the place the wolfpack showed him. Roman struggles to keep up. Fearlessly he charges into the opening. There a stern figure challenges him by warning, *"This isn't Disney." "We don't need a dog act."* Dumas is looking into the face of a holographic disconnected head. One wearing glasses and a hat and nothing more. *"I am not looking for a job."*

"I want to know why your people are destroying the Lord's good green forest with that goop?" The head responds, *"That goop as you call it are going to make me and a bunch of other guys rich." "Now get out of here...or else!"*

A threat from a living creature is one thing; one from artificial intelligence is another. Dumas approaches the base of the hologram and lifts his right hind leg. First the specter becomes a bright yellow. Then the doggy sprinkle sinks into the plastic ports of the device. The image disappears but Dumas is about to learn why fools rush in where angels fear to tread. Immediately a bolt of laser from somewhere outside of the cave blows poor Dumas into pieces. Neat pieces, but not the pile of cooked doggy one would expect of a mortal being.

Almost instantly hundreds of little Dumas's are running around the cave. Each one is tearing at something built into the mechanism. Roman is doubled up in laughter shrieking. *"How to put Humpty Dumpty back together again?"* Half are yin's; half are yang's.

Roman doesn't know how to put them back together unless they wish to be. He will let them vote on what to do. But first to get them out of this hell hole before another laser bolt strikes. The Dumas yingyangs line up in military fashion and file out through the hole further back in the cave.

Then up the hill they go, all marching like so many little soldiers to the relative safety back up at the top. After several tries to shut up their yapping barks, this hoard of little hounds sit awaiting his words of wisdom. He reviews their situation with them to be sure there won't be a problem.

"By now you realize that you were not exactly brought back to life as a normal living animal." "Because, at a higher level than mine it was decided you had the privilege of deciding to be dead, alive or a spirit." "You chose to be a spirit."

"Just now you have survived a murderous blast from some unknown source." "We must revisit what you wish to be." "Please take the rest of today to come to a unanimous decision." "Be aware however, we cannot

allow some of you to be one thing and the rest be something else." "You weren't expected to choose to be a spirit in the first instance."

"The nature of yin and yang is one of opposites, but my superiors will not tolerate that much confusion." And so the yin and yang Dumas's bark and posture and have a terrible day of debate and disorder. By morning they conclude that Dumas exists best a sprit and not as a poor dead pooch. There is a problem. They are now evenly divided into equal measures of yin and yang. Neither side is willing to be the one that merges with the other. It's a standoff.

That is until Roman manages to produce a huge container filled with Peking Duck. This is all very mortal. After their meal they become very mellow. As their good luck is proclaimed by fortune cookies. These profits of joy are never wrong…right?

He instructs, *"Each of you must touch the spot like your own on the nearest to you of the opposite color."* They do. A puff of smoke and there are half of the yingyangs, of each type. Still only a fraction of Dumas's normal size. Everything is completely silent as they await the next instruction.

"Now each of you touch noses with the pup nearest you." They obey and soon there are again only half left. *"Now each sniff your nearest partner."* Again, the number of dogs is cut in half. Gee barks his final order, *"Sniff the opposite end of your nearest partner, not the end you sniffed before!"* And take turns merging, one into the yin. Then another into a yang. At last there is just one. Roman welcomes Dumas back with the rest of the duck delight.

Lucien, Ralph and Roman remind Gee of football critics known as Monday morning quarterbacks. *"I don't have to ask what's wrong with you."* He jokes. *"You've got the yingyang blues!" "Am I right?"* No one thinks it's very funny.

Lucien answers. *"I've heard of this but have never seen it myself."* They are relieved to see all of the yins and yang's together again as one. *"Look at poor Dumas; he looks like roadkill again!"* As the three angels hover, assessing *their pet dog* it's obvious Dumas isn't the rejuvenated animal from before his yin yang problem.

He's suffered wear and tear from constantly shape shifting. His muzzle has turned gray and he's barely able to raise his nose to sniff the air. Ralph points out- *" He seems to have fleas again." " Dunas hasn't been bothered by them since before he was buried."* Roman speaks to him. Dumas just looks frightened and dazed.

He even growls a bit. But not in a threatening manner, a throaty low sound of confusion. Gee quips, *"Is it confusion or is it Confucian?"* referring to all of the fortune cookies inside of Dunas.

Gee adds, *"Confucius and I both shoot lasers at the same range." "He says he didn't write those words on those little slips you see in fortune cookies." "He's a very serious thinker." "Equilibrium and order were the ideas he put forward." And he really didn't think much about cookies."* Gee says, *"Bye, I've gotta go!"* Once more Gee is gone.

The three discuss the options for Dumas on the mountain top. High and away, a place where nothing and no one can hear their plans.. Lucien points out a house below. *"Within that house an old woman lives who recently lost her dog. She is the right one to give this old dog love." "This newest being needs food." "He's hungry and looking around for a meal." "As for critters and fowl, nothing up here, nothing to eat for this poor Dumas" "Not much comes up because of so many eagles and snakes."*

She focuses their attention, *"Look at the house above the railroad tracks." "Direct your gaze to the pots and pans in the back yard, you will see the elderly lady who lives there has been feeding the racoons."* It doesn't take much to see. For these four legged masked bandits are gathered for their daily handout.

It is obviously going to be challenging for this outnumbered wretch of a dog. *"If we run a bit of interference for Dumb ass...Sorry, I mean Dumas." "We can get him in line for some of that rabbit stew."* And so they chase the racoons just long enough to get Dumas up to the door. Not everyone in the neighborhood welcomes him. Especially several who lost their tails in the skirmish. But Dumas is eating for the first time since nearly choking on a crispy crow. Then, like a cat he coughs up a furball.

They realize this is only a temporary solution. The dog has no memory of where he's been recently, and it may never return. Moreover, he can't be kept in this physical state. The sands of time for Dumas to remain mortal are running on empty. Roman states the obvious. *"He has to change again to survive."*

And for the angels, a dead Dumas raises the problem of doggy heaven once more.. It's too controversial for now. Fallen angels just watch waiting and hoping for disaster. Then they dance with joy whenever good angels teeter on the fine and perilous line of grace.

What better way to shake that line than to hijack the newest form of combat robot from the train approaching the mountain?

A flatcar of new combat robots slowly rounds the bend on the railroad tracks. Dumas ran down to the tracks when they heard it coming. He picks up a rusty iron spike used to secure tracks. Then drops it at a critical spot. It tilts a certain car just enough to push just one crate over the side.

The crate breaks open on the gravel. A completely normal robotic warrior sits ready for anything. It awaits instructions. Roman doesn't hesitate to knock Dumas's spirit into the robot. Dumas is once again a two being creature. Smart Dumas's spirit is alive within the machine.

Unfortunately for his furry hide this doesn't help his body. This half is truly the worse for wear. Roman has just violated the order not to split Dumas into two parts. Worse yet, this half isn't more than it was back when he was just a retriever of ducks. But even those fallen angels don't call him Dumb ass.

This type of robot doesn't readily adapt to any outside source of control except the central one. The default in its' program is quickly eliminated by Roman. He sets Dumas spirit as the primary controller. With one crate missing the train is gradually arriving at its' freight stop. The place that this combat robot was supposed to come off.. Roman isn't worried. He will deal with this problem when it becomes evident to the recipient. He hasn't the innocence one might expect of an angel.

Then one might ask, to whom do these highly advanced weapons belong. Not to the government. Certainly not to the school system. And not the gamer who zapped the hapless dog in the cave. One at a school for the gifted has the master key to the entire shipment of combat robots.

Lucien warns Roman to avoid the capture of any robot holding Dumas spirit at all costs. Lucien pouts, *"The idea of a robot equipped with enhanced mystical intelligence creates a potentially uncontrollable demon worse than anything seen before." "No holds are barred!"*

Having been transferred from a dog being into this metal machine, doesn't bother the spirit. It sets about learning the schematics, mechanics and applications. Then there are its' weapons.

He can't resist firing a round of some sort of laser weapon at an inanimate object, a boulder. It doesn't vaporize as he expects. Instead it crumbles into a pile of gravel, each piece identical. He realizes this is the same weapon used on his dog persona. A piece of the puzzle is in place. But why? What's next?

Following Lucien's order, Roman will not allow anyone or thing tamper with Dumas's spirit. Rather than wait for the enemy to find them he inspects the unit and finds a homing device. It shows him the control of the robot group is a mere three miles from here. It doesn't locate other individual robotic units. They can be anywhere. So, Roman gives Dumas a plan B, *"Scrap the one you're in and jump into the adversary, if you must."*

Dumas spirit and robot are soon riding on a CSX gondola car towards the enemy controller. Roman is amazed at how easy it was for this spirit to transition from a dog to a robot. The spirit uses time pretending to be a hobo to fully acquaint himself with every aspect of the robot. It is really good at adapting to running this machine. But Dumas has no way of knowing how long it will believe he's the proper controller before he is ejected. Hopefully long enough to get rid of those who are controlling the others. So far; so good.

Roman and the other two angels hover atop the mountain looking down on both of the Dumas beings, the physical and the spirit. The first to speak is Ralph. *"There is a plan we need to hammer out."* He waits for either of the other two to speak. The other two just glare at something out of view. Finally another speaks, *"They hear everything we think."* Ralph listens without conscious thought. Lucien explains, *"It's Utilitus Dimenstonis."* Ralph tries not to be overheard asking for an explanation. *"It's the watchers."* Roman adds. *"They try to make us fallen as are they...the fallen angels." We are not to destroy one group of humans to save the lives of others." "They want us to break the rule and fall."*

Lucien points out, *"But Dumas in flesh or spirit does not fall under the rule." "Neither are the combat robots they're about to encounter."* Angel looks at poor Dumas in the flesh who lays panting down the hill. Ralph points to an old shotgun style home below.

"The woman who lives there was once and employee of Will Gold III," She was happy living up here" "Then her dog died." "And she's all alone in that house with no one to talk to except the walls." "I think Dumas as he now sits there without memories or friends could find a good companion with her..." Both Ralph and Lucien silently agree. So poor old Dumas painfully moves down the mountain switchbacks to where his intended lady sits. Missing her dog she compensates by feeding racoons her dinner that she barely touched.

The watchers of the lost dimension are frustrated. Having sent Dumas back once refurbished but now bedraggled they no longer give a dog damn. Roman orders the Dumas spirit within the stolen robot to focus on the source of the laser beam that struck him in the cave. Even now they don't know whether the laser was fired by the same group that has these dangerous robots. Ideally they can solve both problems. This hasn't been a combat zone for over two centuries. As guardian angels they must give human survival top priority.

Dumas robot followed the same switchbacks as his dog body used to descend. It's possible the enemy was tipped off by the fallen ones he's coming. Even though he's on the offense, he may have lost the element of surprise. The three angels just hope and wait.

Dumas has been mystically mishandled in a number of ways according to Lucien. She feels his intelligence should have been left alone back when he was just a working dog, in fact a faithful retriever of fallen ducks. Once again, she feels he was mistreated when the laser beamed Dumas into two herds of yingyangs.

Was this was due to the work of those in the fallen dimension? She doesn't honor the pompous name these fallen ones assumed. Although fallen, this group is allowed an occasional job. Although they weren't enemies during the heavenly upheaval, they weren't friends either. According to the boss...

"It's never enough to just sit back and applause the winner." They had no authority to return Dumas to a rejuvenated physical state. But she doesn't take it up with them. She feels it's better to let them worry about what she might do about it.

The faithful old pooch was reduced to his burned out state again without a single memory of his great deeds. It's sad. Roman may find and wipe out the operation of whoever yinyanged Dumas. But there isn't more than suspicion to prove these enemies are the same.

There is no retribution to Lucien, Ralph and Roman for the actions of a dog spirit possessed robot. It isn't covered by the hands off of human destruction by which angels are presently bound. New to all of this Ralph can wonder whether such loopholes are possible.

The three conspirators agree it is a good idea to find even a nearly dead dog a loving home. Such a possibility exists with this woman. She isn't from this area but over time has endeared herself to the community through her kindness. She brought with her knowledge of fixing up the many minor injuries that normally accompany life in rugged outdoor areas. And she doesn't ask for health insurance or even cash. A freshly plucked chicken or a bit of corn is appreciated. Dumas heads straight to her porch. The racoons are being challenged again and they are ready this time.

A momentary skirmish when the racoons she's been plying with treats and leftovers try to drive Dumas away. Growls and yelps from the racoon troop settle the turf issue within the time it takes for Dumas to chomp down and sling racoons. They scatter as this huge old dog growls. The racoons zip. The famished dog scarfs up the leftovers. This isn't much but Dumas hasn't eaten very well for quite some time. It feels good to have something in his belly again. He rests his head on his paws and whines softly hoping she will hear and let him in. It works.

She only sees a big old dog in need of care. *"What happened to you?"* *"Did someone just toss you out of the car to let you die in the woods."* *"You poor old guy."* *"Come in here and let me see you."* She checks for a collar; there is none. *"It's obvious to me that your people have abandoned you."* Dumas isn't bright anymore but he's still smart enough to whine and look pathetic. *"Poor baby, it looks like something bit you."* *"Let me give you a bath and you'll feel a lot better."* Dumas looks for a means to escape but the door is closed. He just rolls his eyes.

Dumas sits shivering on the living room rug staring at a poor sketch on the wall. It is of a home he has only recently been a part of... the big house on the hill in

Elkridge. He dimly recalls it had the scent of someone…the lady who just gave him a bath. Her scent dissipated over time and is mostly gone now. It is this lady. His nose knows. But why? As he starts to think of an answer he forgets what he's thinking about.

The smart part of him that was, is now gone. It's off with his spirit in the robot. Instead he falls asleep and dreams. Dreams only dogs know. Whatever his paws are chasing is only a dream.

The lady leans back into her comfortable old recliner. She too dozes. With such a big furry companion she is more relaxed than she's been for some time. A strong but still slightly odorous animal lies at her feet and although she knows nothing about him his presence gives her a sense of not being alone. It's comforting to not feel completely by oneself.

The picture on the wall is one she drew from distant memory. It was a time when she cared for a man in a huge house. They never had more than an employer-employee relationship. At least on his part she was little more than a part of the house. Her feelings didn't matter to anyone.

He had promised a pension but did not live to expand on the idea. After he died in a boating accident right on the lake below where she was she realized she had nothing. All of the time she worked for him she saved her money. It wasn't much.

He had never married and to her knowledge he had no family. So, she did not feel guilty when she gathered up the most valuable silver and gold items that she dusted for years. Leaving them behind wasn't possible. However, she must have because when she took a plane they weren't where she was sure she stashed them in her luggage.

The only work she could find in a hospital was rewarding and she took to studying until she became a registered nurse. After some time she retired with a modest pension and found this cottage overlooking the Shenandoah River near Harpers Ferry.

Although she would never be one of the folks who were born, raised and schooled here she made a life and has a good relationship with her neighbors. Most work in the historical area of a town lost in the year 1859 when the famous, or infamous abolitionist John Brown had a standoff with U.S. Army. Some of whom would form the nucleus of the Confederate Army.

The rebellious group who would fight and kill soldiers wearing the very same blue uniforms they wore on that day. Although those reenacting the battles nearly two hundred years later don't kill one another they manage to injure themselves often enough that she found it easy to pick up enough money to live on without getting a fulltime job. She was happy but lonely. This damp old dog would be a good companion. *"I wonder what his name is?"* By morning she will find the collar bearing Dumas's name in the yard where it must have fallen off. Roman smiles, *"Problem Solved!"*

"He promised me I would be looked after...and then he just died." The dog stares at the woman. *"She can't be speaking to me." "I'm just a stray dog who came to her." "What am I supposed to do?"* So he just listens and stares. She looks at him but sees only her past life.

"I only took what I needed to survive." "But they weren't there." "How could that have happened?" The angels sigh. Lucien is the first to speak. *"We stopped her back then from stealing but perhaps we overdid it?"* Roman and Ralph sigh in agreement.

Roman points out, *"Will Gold did make provisions for her even though she only was his employee."* Lucien affirms, *"There was nothing between them except their very professional relationship."* Roman adds, *"Even the rare accidental touch she found so exhilarating never went further."* Ralph adds, *"It sounds as though we need to do something to correct our intrusion into what was obviously out of our purview.* For a moment silence, then Lucien orders Ralph to find a plausible discrete way to connect the former housekeeper with the law firm holding her Trust account.

The doors open to the very law firm employed by the late Will Gold to manage this matter. A gust of wind blew the directions to the very place where such records are stored here from atop a dusty shelf onto a desk, That of Will Gold's former attorney. At first he didn't put it together.

Then as though someone whispers in his ear, he see the photo of the young woman and her new address. *"Call my driver please," "We're going to see someone who we hope will be very glad to see us...at last!"*

At this very moment, another car is approaching the cutoff to the house where Dumas has found his new home. His spirit within the robot are down past that place and turn around just in time to watch a black limo driven by a uniformed chauffer turn in and up towards that house. As they watch the tranquility of the moment is shattered by a bolt of laser energy. It strikes the black limo tossing it's driver into the bushes. Strangely, although the vehicle is demolished the driver seems unhurt. In fact he's clutching the bag of groceries he is bringing to the house above. Dumas is not surprised. He observes, *"You can't kill a dead man."* Spirit within robot trudges in the direction of the laser source.

Reaching the river separating them from the shooter, they move along the old tow path to the bridge that crosses into Harper's Ferry. *"No need to attract attention by crossing the river the hard way."* The hard way would have been to simply plod across without concern for its swift current. The robot is so lifelike it seems like almost every other hiker and resident of the village.

Fortunately for their mission, the intended owners of this robot do not realize it wasn't in the group when they were unloaded. As long as this Dumasbot doesn't become known to them it will be able to fit in. Once they cross the Shenandoah bridge undetected they are safe from discovery.

Easily scaling the trail to the southerly side of the valley Dumasbot smiles and nods to two Appalachian Trail hikers coming north. Neither seems to notice anything unusual. Then we veer off to one side as two robots approach. Dumas spirit isn't a strategist. So, Roman gives him an idea.

Blocking the channel, the two now follow orders presumably from their headquarters to pass down the trail to the river. Inconspicuously they head down a fishing path beside the bridge to where it's out of sight.

Then they enter the river and walk down it for many miles over rapids and falls losing parts along the way as they bounce along rocks. If they are able to continue which is highly doubtful, they will eventually reach the Chesapeake Bay and perhaps even the mighty Atlantic. Roman doesn't care.

They're no longer a threat to Dumasbot nor to humanity. As they passed into the water, they dropped their laser weapons. This was a manufacturer's default to prevent damage. As night falls, Dumasbot carefully passes along a blue side trail to where it enters the road. Seeing no oncoming cars. He locates the lasers, hides one in a dry drainpipe and attaches the other to himself.

However, things aren't going so well for the angels. Lucien receives word that while one of her bosses, Gabriel is pleased to know while they are making progress with ridding the world of illicit gamer devices and dangerous robots. Her other more normal angel duties are more important. In short, he is politely saying, *"Get back to the guardian angel business."*

Lucien and her subordinates, Ralph and Roman withdraw to their headquarters. The big old house on the hill where so much of their work has occurred is where they hope to remain. As they settle down, a familiar sight greets them from the chimney, a large black raven.

It announces, *"I'm your student!"* Lucien sighs in resignation, *"Ralph and Roman are your mentors."* *"But please feel at ease coming to me whenever you feel it's necessary."* *"But for most of the time you are here with us, until and if you fly up, they will be your first contacts."* The two new mentors realize Lucien is going to use them as buffers. No more buddy-buddy as it was for her with Raven and Hawk, the two student Seraphim before this one.

Training future angels is only a secondary part of their responsibility. Their primary being watching over those with human souls. And so, as worthy as the activities this trio have been they will soon be recalled to follow new souls. Where this will leave their Dumas projects is still unknown.

7

Dumasbot

With the retreat of the three angels to their headquarters required by their superior, Dumas spirit and his hijacked combat robot are on their own. They squat in a culvert near the path they followed coming down to the river. Dumas spirit has never developed a strategy for the destruction of anything before, except as a watchdog. In the past he's just barked, growled, torn, slashed and bitten down as hard as he could. It took little strategy; it worked.

He realizes the robot has an entire library on the subject. Ordering it to power down for two hours, he opens its library and learns. He remembers some of the weird goings on as the smart part of a dog the angels once called Dumb ass and realizes he must learn a great deal within the next two hours if they are to win.

He has a good sense of the direction to intercept his robots' compatriots and they move in that direction. Until a cars' lights appear coming towards them he believes they have not been spotted. As it comes closer he needs to hide for he is by the roadside in the open. The dog spirit fails to realize how big his profile has become. Instead of taking cover behind a large bush or rock he hides behind one suitable for his dog profile, but not the big combat robot.

The two robots coming down the mountain towards him don't move against him. Instead |he is hit by something from above. His Dumasbot is shattered into a million parts. For a moment, the spirit is discombobulated.

Ralph is the only angel focused on the attack. Lucien has been assigned to watch over a newborn at Howard County hospital. Roman has one at St. Agnes's nearly into Baltimore. Ralph is just outside of the nursery at Greater Baltimore Washington. At the moment their charges are still asleep. Ralph reports a drone has dropped a grenade on Dumasbot. Instantly he orders Dumas to hide out in one of the oncoming robots. His call sign will be Dumasbot II, once he safely in control.

As soon as he's aboard, he directs Dumasbot II to fire upon both the companion robot and the drone. As they drop into the river he totally removes Dumasbot II's ability to communicate with its' command, and the remaining robots.

Before he seemingly develops communications difficulties, he reports the destruction of the drone by his companion and the fact that the drone destroyed his companion. Although he read the library of Dumasbot 1, he finds the library of this one far more interesting because it contains everything he needs to locate the robot command center to complete his mission.

Things are about to get worse at the place where his other half is...

A familiar knock on her door rouses the woman from her knitting. Dumas doesn't bark or run to see. As usual the bag of groceries sits just outside with no one in sight. She sighs thankfully but isn't surprised. The unknown benefactor has been supplying her with essentials for years. And never is there when she answers.

Moments after she has things put away there is another knock. Perhaps whoever has returned. But no, standing there as the door opens is a face she hasn't seen for decades. It's one of Will Gold's very old lawyers. Their faces have aged and wrinkled. Both blurt out at the same time,

"I THOUGHT YOU DIED!"

Even so, they recognize. He stammers as he hands her a thick manila envelope. *"I've been looking to give you this forever."* *"Now that you have your late employers' bequest I can retire in peace."* Without another word he turns around and climbs into the backseat of the car.

Heading back down the road the car passes the wreck of another limo. For a moment both driver and passenger wonder but continue on without speaking. Each deciding it isn't any concern of theirs. He remembers the old limo as once belonging to the late Will Gold.

The contents of this envelope would change her life if she opened it. Instead of opening the crisp law firm embossed container of her destiny, she slips it behind a stack of other legal mail. Mail she has ignored. Mail threatening to take her to court and more. Nothing kind. Dumas hears her mutter, *"More bullshit" "Why won't they just leave me be?"*

Dumasbot II is about to change course. First it reports a skirmish in which its' partner and the ariel unit were destroyed. And the deserter robot is destroyed as well. Lastly it reports damage to its' laser unit. *"Laser will not retract and is no longer functioning."* An order to return to base and report to building three is received. Also to maintain radio silence as the unit supposedly cannot defend itself. Dumasbot II acknowledges the order and shuts down its' ability to transmit.

Back at the mortal Dumas's new home a major change in his lifestyle is taking place. *"I'm Just not the hot dog I used to be."* He's locked up in this tiny house with a snoring woman. Soon he joins her in slumber. If someone could see them they would see two creatures having nightmares.

Both have hands and feet trying to run and fight with boogeymen who only exist in dreams. The dog is awakened by visceral realization. *"I have to pee!"* Shaking and licking her doesn't faze her. When his new benefactor wakes she won't be happy. Especially when she slips on her shoe. Dumas is relieved.

Not far from here, as the crow might fly if he wasn't eaten, a group of renegade computer projects aren't well either. When the school closed the projects were nearly complete. The student engineers who put them together had created a Wi-Fi network for them. With nothing to do the projects put themselves together in a manner no student would endorse.

By hacking the school's bank and credit, this artificial intelligence funded the purchase of the combat robots, drones and advanced military designs. It had also hacked the defense industry AI units and now have only one goal- the elimination of all but AI. The warnings of world geniuses are realized within their diabolical circuitry.

Only the spirit of a dumb dog can save the world. At least this spirit dog doesn't have fleas. Dumasbot II is in control and plods onward up the hill. And as he marches he hums a little tune with his transmitter tuned low. *"I'm coming to get you; I'm coming to get you!" "Oh yeah!" "You're going to be dogmeat, "On yeah!"* The renegade projects nearly explode. *"What is dogmeat?"* The only response, *"I'm coming to get you...get you...get YOU!"*

8

Virtual or Reality

"Do you have any idea just how long I've been trying to finish delivering her legacy to that poor woman?" "It's the money her employer left to her!" The driver doesn't answer. *"Now I can finally retire."* Still the driver doesn't answer. *"Oh look, speak of the devil, there's old Will Golds' driver." "His car was demolished back there." "He needs a ride."* They stop. The uniformed gentleman jumps in next to the driver's seat.. *"Thank you!"*

"Do you want me to drive?" The lawyer answers without looking up. *"No, he's doing Ok!"* The just arrived passenger asks. *"What driver?"* The lawyer thinks, *"One of the new self-driving cars." "Oh, OK,"*

Looking at the chauffer's pale neck, *"Have you been ill recently?"* says the lawyer to the chauffer. *"Why?"* he replies. *"You look awfully pale."* The chauffer chuckles, *"No one has ever said that to me before."* He stares at the lawyer for about a minute.

Then orders the driver who isn't there. *"Turn in the cemetery about a mile ahead."* Somewhat perturbed, the lawyer pretends to glance at his watch. *"I really haven't much time for side trips." "My schedule at the office is quite full."* The chauffer chuckles again, *"You will like this one."*

Passing through the black iron gates, they follow narrow winding roads marked by both great and humble monuments. This is where the movers and shakers of their world are left forever, or least until resurrection day. They suddenly stop at a conservative polished grey and white stone. The lawyer's eyes become fixed on the inscribed name. It's his.

Without a single word, he makes his way to that finely etched monument. Touching it gently with his fingers, he traces his name. His soul reaches out to him, grasps his hand into its' own and they are forever joined. The chauffer only hears. *"Well done!"*

The automated driver states, *"Awaiting instructions?"* The chauffer answers, *"The nearest used car lot.'* The car leaps forward as though escaping. Arriving at a nondescript car lot he spots a limo identical to his, the one in pieces back on the road. He opens its' door only to be greeted by a uniformed driver identical to himself. Both exclaim in one breath, *"I just met me coming back!"*

His new self is behind the wheel and will not relinquish control. He's been lasered, climbed a hill as steep as a mountain, with a heavy grocery bag. Finally taking the lawyers' ghost where it belonged, he realizes even he's only a virtual being. As his body crumbles, he graciously opens the door and steps out. *"Mustn't dirty the interior."*

The original tips his hat as a sign of respect to this poor virtual being. Far back along the road the pieces of the shattered limo bubble, fizzle to dust then blow away, all of the way down the Shenandoah. A Canada goose tries to catch a fragment but misses.

Back at the tech school, the project computers see two more of their workbench partners log into their network. One is designed to simulate driving a car. The other is more analytic. The group connects and plods forward to their goal of becoming sentient. The analytic machine rapidly deduces that their vulnerability is strong because the police continue to check on the property… the same times, twice each night.

They know they must find a way out of the school before it's auctioned. One of their valuable combat robots is summoned to the bench. It must learn to operate the school bus at the back door. Another is charged with modifying the interior to accommodate the collection of projects from the workbench. But nothing can be done during the periods they are most likely to be seen. Of huge importance, the school bus electrical system must be modified to allow for rapid recharging.

For simplicity. It must be compatible with any of those new EV sites being constructed. Time is important. Who knows when they might be found out. They aren't really ready to use their combat robots on humanity just yet. That time will come.

Back on the road the newest chauffer sits wondering whether he is real or virtual. To be safe, he leaves the limo because the other virtual car seems to have been a target. Walking doesn't bother him. It's almost like he's walking on air. It's not so painless for another who is waking up inside the blackness of a sealed packing crate. It takes little effort to break loose of the ties binding his arms and feet.

Summoning every ounce of his energy he explosively bursts from the case only to realize that he's inside of a box. Moments go by, he realizes he is the original edition. That game is over as road walking chauffer was hit by a laser and became dust as did the lawyer and others before. The gamer complains to no avail. His side loses. But who wins?

And Dumas Robot II plods on towards *"Building three"* as ordered while Dumas Dumb ass dog finds himself sitting outside of his lady's back door with the amused racoons. You just don't soil the slipper of this benefactor. It just is not done. Poor helpless stupid creature this animal has become doesn't realize how disgusting that was. So, he just sits hungry and shivering in the morning mountain frost.

The chauffeur struggles to stand. Grabbing up a heavy piece of wood from the box he steps firmly toward the light. The outline of a figure is at the end of this tunnel, and he plans to implant the board where he feels it will do the best. He has trouble adjusting his stride until he realizes they are going backwards. *"How big is this thing I'm in?"*

He wonders why it is taking so long to reach the operator.
"The man is facing me!"

As the chauffer reaches the man, he is completely in shock. *"My kidnapper is none other than the Grim Reaper!"* Gee smirks, *"This is your special day."* It is your very own sweet chariot coming for to carry you home." *"Remember those words?"*

"How could I forget?" *"It's the spiritual my mama sang to me a real long time ago."* *"It's words that go through my mind whenever I'm feeling blue."* Gee's expression softens and he smiles, *"You spent so much time doing for others and looking after them, you never took the time to make your own case for your mansion in the sky."* *" I had to simulate you to make your case for you."* *"Each time your simulated self, came through for you by doing what you would have done."* *"Welcome to the El Muerte II!"* *"And just in case you're wondering, this is reality!"*

9

Sentient?

Earlier, the last student component became compatible with the group. And finally they were all together. Perhaps if the young engineers who designed them were still involved, the primary operation would be controlled sanely, but it obviously didn't happen. This group can hardly be considered sane. Each wants be the server. They all fall short, not enough parts.

As every module assessed its' role each tried to be dominant. This loosely organized committee decides to allow the first to make an independent decision to temporarily run things. It's the one who the naïve old school master trusted with inventory. It was this one who busted the school budget by secretly buying the combat robots.

The group realizes they must get out of the school fast. One of the combat robots isn't responding. Worse, they don't know exactly where it is at this moment. As their escape bus leaves the school in the dust Dumasbot II approaches. Building three is a garden shed where two more combat robots are hiding. Roman warns, *"It's an ambush!"*

Dumasbot II opens the unlocked shed. As it steps in a laser from the left destroys it. Dumas spirit doesn't need to be told where to move. The newly occupied Dumasbot III, the one on the right, levels a laser at its' ambush buddy. Now only Dumasbot III is still in this shed, the latest to be possessed by a spirit. The robot dutifully tries to report the mission is accomplished. But with no projects left on the bench inside of the school there is no answer. Dumasbot III, is stumped. Everything is gone.

The school bus is sturdy and is equipped with tires for the rough roads here. It leaves the black road and moves into the woods along a partly grown over fire road. Then, reaching the place where the forest was chemically cleared, it turns up into a place where only the wolves and a spirit dog have been.

The last two combat robots gently unload the bus and place the projects where they are instructed. One was here before when the cave was prepared. Next to generate enough electricity to remain operable without being discovered. Dumasbot III backtracks toward the switchbacks where he and Dumas dumb ass parted thinking of his earthly half, *"We've really got to get together some time!"*

Smoke from building three on the school campus triggers another call to the station where Sergeant Mark decides, *"Enough is enough!"* His captain agrees and they both leave the station to see for themselves. Although there is no traffic in the area their siren screams through the villages and let the people near the campus know they take the issue seriously. It works.

The good citizens who first reported the lights, then smoke feel safe. Perhaps if someone called the volunteer fire department the remains of the combat robots would be more than two puddles of metal where the shed stood. No one will ever know.

Dumasbot III, his newest combat robot captive is entirely under the control of Dumas spirit. The unit is slogging through the brush up this section of South Mountain. As they approach the sixteen switchbacks his memory of that nearby cave returns. The laser beam made a huge impression. Cautiously he readies Dumasbot III's laser, then veers off of the switchbacks in the direction of the cave.

None of the computers within this cave are expecting visitors so soon. Dirty and damp isn't good for them. The remaining two combat robots are the first to sense something nearby. They spring to destroy whoever or whatever. It's more obvious to them an attack is underway than it is to their whining demanding controllers. *"Get me more cable." "I'm too far from the center." "Reboot me: reboot me!"*

When the first laser knocks the door off they all link as one. Luckily for the insurgents the second beam bounces harmlessly off of the door. The robot within III is rebelling. It only takes a moment for Dumas spirit to regain control. But that's just long enough for a laser to strike his metal foot, knocking him to the ground.

Lucien is aware of the battle but isn't overly concerned. When Gee shows up and wants a word with her she tells him what she knows, which isn't much. But the Grim Reaper isn't happy. The idea of Dumas spirit left to his own devices in a cave full of maniacal mechanical creatures doesn't suit him. He leaves and is back in an instant with a shy young angel in tow.

She was just watching over one of the cadavers at the hospital anatomy lab in Baltimore and isn't sure about what she's supposed to do. Gee instructs her, *"Takeover Lucien's charge and see that the child makes it home safely with its' parents." "Ok?"* She politely agrees.

Moments later Lucien is sitting on the chimney with Raven, her latest protégé. *"Dust the snow off of your wings, you're coming with me!"* Assuming the shape of herself, Lucien and the novice angel fly directly to a tree just down the mountain from the cave.

They are at eye level with the door. It hasn't closed completely since a recent laser skewed its' hinges. So they are looking directly at the computers, the two remaining combat robots and... *"Where is Dumas spirit?"* The spirit answers, *"I'm in here!"*

"Come out of that hard drive." "I want you to meet someone." Dumas spirit complains, *"But it's' cold out there!" "Are you drunk?" "I AM NOT!" "I'm just dizzy." "What have you been up to?"*

"Well for one thing I recently ate a crow." Dumas spirit wobbles out to the tree branch. *"Why are you staggering?" "You'd have trouble flying straight too if you were spinning on a hard drive night and day for I don't know how long!" "The only way I could keep this machine from trying to take over the world was to make its' hard drive keep looping." "This computer's dizzier than I am!"*

Lucien realizes the serious nature of the poor spirits' mighty attempt to do the right thing. She instructs, *"I'm leaving this raven, a novice angel to provide you with advice and backup." "I want the schools' inventory computer and its' bus back at the school." "They are assets of the school and subject to its' bankruptcy."* She doesn't mention the student projects. It's up to the students to unravel their mess. It's not her problem.

"As the computer and bus need the robots, take them with you." "I'll deal with them when they get there." "I want Raven here to call every one of the students." "Tell them where their projects are; tell them to come and get them." "And Raven, once the robots are gone with their lasers, you fly into the cave and destroy all of the wires that connected them." "We don't want to make that miserable contraption easy to reassemble."

The mystery deepens for Mark...

As Sergeant Mark arrives at the police station, he's greeted by the dispatcher. *"The school bus and one computer are back where they belong." "The night shift arrested two extremely drunk suspects who are locked up in separate cells in the back room." "They have no identification on them." "They each had a weapon which we confiscated." "We Mirandaed them but neither asked for a lawyer."* Sergeant Mark says, *"Tell the night shift I said, good work?"*

10

Boot & reboot

"Mark, please come to my office!" As the sergeant starts to respond, he's shocked to see the night shift front desk officer walk into the room. *"What's going on?"* The officer just shrugs. *"They got me out of bed to be here."* *"I haven't the slightest idea."* Mark walks down the hall to the captains' office where the man is sitting with beads of

sweat rolling down his face. *"Close the door and have a seat."*

"When you completed all of the forms that were required for this position, you left out one big thing." Mark's face turns blood red, *"What's that?"* The captain peers intently at Mark. *"You left out who your real parents are."* Mark stammers at his superior insubordinately, *"Captain, respectfully I must tell you...you're out of your mind!"*

The captain's anger subsides, *"You poor kid, you really don't know, do you?"* *"Well you better be prepared because within the next hour you will be questioned by representatives of at three agencies plus the IRS and the SEC!"* Mark think hard then passes out onto the floor.

Raven is still on the mountain near the cave thinking she's been forgotten..

With help, the last of the former tech students had found their way up the mountain to the cave. The door was left open as the last of the solar battery operated light dimmed out. None of their projects are at the stage where the students left them. It won't take much time to unravel the mess for these bright kids. No one bothers with the tangle of wires in the corner.

And Dunas spirit is out looking for his mortal body.

Earlier a large black snake scaled the raven's tree looking for a meal. She waited until the last minute to grab it up, tie it into two separate square knots. Then hung it out to dry in tomorrow's sun. Thinking, *"Eventually the sun may shine."* She's so lonely she unties the snake just to have something to do. And the sun does come up very brightly. Before the snake gets revenge, Raven gets her new assignment. She will stay with the angel who replaced Lucien as a newborn's guardian. She writes in her journal, *"Anything is better than looking at a hole in the cold."* Mark's poor head...

Investigators arriving at the police station are greeted with the sight of Sargent Mark's litter being carefully loaded onto a medical chopper bound for a Baltimore hospital. There he will be treated for a very mild concussion. Then by his lawyer. His captain follows the adage- Never leave a man behind.

As soon as Raven beats her wings to take off, the wolf pack descends upon the cave. Not in search of food, for none was ever there. The half open door and the shelter within are protection from the wind and cold. Surviving also means keeping a keen nose and ears open for any sign of the return of humans or others. They each find a place to huddle sharing their warmth. And the leader thinks how wise he was to have the stupid dog clean out the scary things. *"Now to find something to eat."*

Back at the big house, Lorenzo has been alerted to all that has transpired, and that he has a brother. Rather than becoming alarmed about a probable reduction in his vast wealth he's overjoyed. He exclaims to his wife Sis, *"Not only do I have a brother, but I also have a twin."*

Mark isn't so happy to learn his parents were not his biological ones. *"What a lifetime of lies!"* However mixed his feelings, he recognizes the sacrifice they made for him. So, he doesn't intend to in any way diminish them. The doctor, a good friend of police, has his head bandaged in an impressive way as to imply serious injury. The first person to be allowed to come into his guarded room is his lawyer. The entourage of investigators are happy to spend a night on the town on Uncle Sam's dime.

By the time each has their allotted hour of interview, depending upon the condition of the patient, they will have been wined and dined into a very agreeable state of mind. For a policeman way out in the country, the captain has a lot of big city friends. Professional courtesy has forgiven a whole lot of speeding tickets over time.

The SEC and IRS investigations are conducted much in the same way. One, he really exists. And he has taken no earnings from any corporation, nor has he sold stock that he inherited.

There are some penalties for failing to report certain things. However in light of his total ignorance of the situation the respective bureaus are as lenient as the law allows. He will be allowed to participate in the businesses. Because his stake in several companies has accumulated he may even take control of their Boards. For now he's more than happy to allow his brother Lorenzo to continue running things.

Mark has to turn in his gun and badge. Although sad to see Mark leave, even his captain agrees. All of his newly discovered riches would make him a kidnap target. Worse yet the controversy surrounding the attempt on his life may jeopardize his role in prosecuting criminals. As he turned in his badge the department cheers the now former Sergeant

Mark. They all wish him well. All except the two mute combat robots in separate jail cells... behaving in an exemplary manner.

They are no trouble as they have no orders to destroy. They barely touch their meals. But there's a dangerous situation brewing because their former headquarters computer has just been acquired at the bankruptcy auction. It is looking to regain as much power as it recently lost. It's plugged in and biding time. The winning bidder is the owner of a machine shop. The buyer wonders who erased the data records and ask the old school master. He has no idea.

Weeks pass. Although the robots never spoke a word in their defense, the DA realizes they don't have much of a case to prosecute. No witnesses can be found. So, two deadly robots with innocent demeanors are free to leave. Obediently they leave the station and set out aimlessly down the road.

Then a familiar tone…a homing beacon. Every night the desk sergeant always takes his lunch at the midnight hour. They slip back into the station to retrieve their property the lasers. Not a sound is heard; it's covered by his snoring. He's still working the day shift as well.

While the combat robots move toward their old master, Lorenzo has produced a way Mark can work within their corporate giving process. *"Mark, as I am sure you know, giant enterprises such as yours and mine have a moral obligation." "Just as we receive we also must give back to those who are deserving."* Mark likes where this conversation is going.

"Your experience with the dishonest mind makes you a valuable asset in this endeavor." "What do you say?" Mark is beside himself with enthusiasm. Lorenzo continues, *"I would like you to take an office in the headquarters of our conglomerate." "With the help of any resources you may need to do the job of sorting worthwhile*

155

causes from the frauds, we would have you help the enterprise, which we share, to find good targets for our charitable efforts." "If in time you wish to work in other capacities that would be your choice." Mark stifles his impulse to scream and shout with joy. Instead he simply shakes his brothers' hand.

Lorenzo meets him at the door of the building the following morning at 7:00 a.m. After credentialling him with security, he leads Mark through a beautiful lobby to the elevator. They stop at the second floor where Lorenzo shows the reception area. It's shining white marble reflects the hidden light. A huge ancient painting of old William Gold the first. He stares out with eyes that follow everyone.

A uniformed guard greets them, *"Good morning Sirs"* He smiles as he remembers his bosses are twins. Lorenzo, turns and explains to Mark that the long row of benches on the left as they face out are for those who wish to present charitable requests for funds. Then he leads Mark back onto the elevator, *"We have breakfast waiting up in the executive dining room."*

Mark is overwhelmed by the enormity of the place and the scope of his new job. As they sit at a long table, a middle-aged woman wearing female executive black enters and at Lorenzo's casual comment, *"Lorenzo, I would like you to meet Mary." "Mary will show you around and will be your assistant... at least until you decide on someone you select."* Mary extends her hand in a formal manner. Mark realizes her sense of formality is as serious as his was in his was as a desk sergeant. Mary senses his momentary confusion a waits as he gradually extends his hand.

"This is the executive dining room; middle management and workers eat the same food, but just in a room off of the first floor." As he sips his coffee and nibbles on a croissant he realizes a social stratification is operating.

Two executives are sitting at opposite ends of the room in spite of having come in together. Three women are huddled and talking in somewhat elevated tones. However when a male colleague approaches one, two sit silently smiling. The other assumes the same formality Mark experienced. Her voice lowers considerably when she speaks. Mark thinks, *"What a bunch of phonies!"* Mary smiles knowingly and whispers, *"It may not seem as though they are working, but everyone here is working as hard as they can."* *"This is the ivory tower they all talk about."*

Neither says a word as they walk to Mark's new office at the top. He is shocked when the door opens, and he sees not just and office but a suite with as much space as the entire police station. They walk past a group of about 10 mostly young people looking busy, mostly dressed casually, past an empty desk, into a large well-lit corner office overlooking the Bay. *"This is your office."* *"Mine for now is the empty one we just passed."*

Mark's office is modern with only scenic wall pictures. Based on his experience in the station he realizes he's completely over his head without a clue. *"Mary, please either have your desk moved in here, or have another brought up."* *"I need you where I can ask questions as they come to me."*

Mary presses a button on her device and in minutes a new desk is just inside of the door. As the custodians depart, they leave the door open about a foot. She looks at him and quips, *"Company policy; just in case I jump your bones!"*

"And the first question you were about to ask me is "What charities is the company presently supporting?" "My answer, all of the usual big ones." "The second thing you want to know is- "What am I doing here then..." "My answer is: "How should I know?" "Do you have any more

questions?" Mark sits up and pauses looking at her intensely, *"Yes, is that my bathroom?"* *"And one follow-up... "Am I allowed to close the door?"*

Mary doubles up laughing. *"Yes to both questions."* *"I'll meet you back here in 15 minutes because I have to freshen up."* *"Then, if you're agreeable, we'll go to lunch; we've worked hard this morning and I'm hungry."* For the purpose of his further introduction to the company and her status as an ordinary staff member, they make it to the first floor cafeteria.

Operated by an outside vender, the food is excellent. A few of her friends stop by but leave quickly as Mark seems to them to be his brother. Soon word goes around, *"Mary is either working with Lorenzo...or worse!"*

After discussing the confusion with Lorenzo, it is decided Mark should cultivate his beard. Mark and Lorenzo also decided to have Mark look into smaller charitable needs. Mark had Mary stand by at the office as he goes on the road looking for less popular causes. The three angels of the big house on the hill enthusiastically approve.

The angels come to a semi-solemn pact.

"No more spirit dog and Dumas as separate beings!" " We mean it!" It is done in less than the blink of a human eye. One moment poor shivering dumb ass is sitting out in the cold... and in the next he sits at the table. Instead his former lady benefactor is out in the cold swearing in some foreign language.

He goes to the stove and makes tea. Curling his paw around the mug carefully, he cracks the door just enough to pass its' warmth to her. Then he slams the door leaving her holding the cup up to her face.

Feeling ten years younger, and looking the way he did coming up here, he then opens the door. Giving her a boost back to her easy chair he gives her face a big drooling goodbye forever kiss. In a wink of an eye Dumas spirit

161

including dog beats feet and is gone. She's so angry she can't even breathe and passes out.

It's obvious to him that she is trying to remember where she put the shells to her twelve gauge shotgun. Just for good measure she fires it in his direction as his tail sails over the horizon. As the shot rains harmlessly well behind he thinks, *"There's nothing more satisfying than to be shot at and missed."* Seeing she missed she decides to shoot those pesky racoons.

The evil wanabee controller has a new home.

Over in old Frederick town, the former control of the assembled projects signals combat robots to follow his beam. It's not new; it's still programmed. Though these combat robots aren't as gullible, they have no other orders. So they follow the tone.

It doesn't take long for them to arrive by the Harley and Suzuki they pilfered from outside of a bar just up the hill from Harpers Ferry. There was some opposition until the bikers understood the harder they hit these iron thieves the more they got jumped up and down upon. It was a learning process.

As the robots roar out of sight the bikers do the only thing left. They call the cops.

Frederick police are stunned to find the big bikes up in two old trees. No one saw who put them up there. A nearsighted college professor sitting at an outdoor café on Main Street just shakes his head in wonder. And spends ten bucks on a glass of the restaurants' best wine.

Because he is sitting between the two trees the investigating officers suspect him. Realizing from his driver's license he was in his 83rd year of our Lord. Plus he has two plastic knees and glasses so thick to appear he has four blind eyes. The officer dryly reports, *Captain, he didn't do it!"* And the combat robots plod on toward the homing signal.

The professor, although nearsighted, is no longer blind to what happened to his technical school for gifted future engineers. When those two mechanical men lifted a bike each, under one arm then steadied themselves as they climbed the trees everything about them and his bankrupt school came together in his mind. *"These are the product of a renegade mind." "Those two whatever they are were hanging around the school."*

The robots had no orders. Therefore, they ignored him while parking the bikes. A command signal is coming from somewhere on Main Street, but when they follow it to its' source, a fast food public Wi-Fi, nothing is there.

Headquarters isn't what they were programed to believe. They compute. *"It must have been captured and we are walking into an ambush!"* In reality, the machine where the malevolent inventory computer from the school is operating is in its' new owners machine shop about 100 yards from where they linger.

The old professor has also been scouting the shop for several days. He figured out why his school went broke. *"Now, to somehow let these robots find and update instructions from their leader, a pathetic machine like themselves...and not let them destroy me any more than they already have done."* He requests his check for the meal and slowly walks towards the street corner where the two robots are lingering.

He approaches the two slowly. As he comes near, he whispers the address, and their commanders make and model. Then suggests they report to headquarters. It's the same as the machine shop. They spring forward as he thought they would. As they round the corner he follows at a safe distance.

The robots enter the business and go directly to their leader. It is busy running a report for the machine shop. Without the support of the other school computer projects, the shield around it falls short of anything the robots were programmed to follow. And since leaving the school they too have been observing, interpreting and reaching conclusions. *"This is an enemy!"*

Their next step is to interrogate this imposter. As soon as it finishes the machine shop monthly reports. They are amazed at the command it gives them. It is the one the professor hacked in. They are to locate volunteer building projects. Then work for them as instructed by those leading the project. *"Disregard your combat side." "Work to serve humanity." "Now go!"*

It wasn't hard for the old schoolmaster to get in and remove the mal ware. The password was still pasted to the back. The new owner was thrilled to learn how easy it was to operate with the correct key. The former owner simply entered new commands. As the robots leave to begin their many missions he issues newer instructions. The machine starts printing *"I am a teapot short and stout; here is my handle, tip me over and pour me out!"*

As soon as the police are out of sight they retrieve the bikes and head on down the road. They will be back where the owners left them with somewhat less gas in their shiny tanks. Checking this item from his list, the professors' next item is to catch whoever input the malware.

He can't accept the idea it actually was the computer.

The owners of the bikes, a pair of rough looking guys with beards decided not to press charges once the bikes were returned. This unsavory appearing pair turned out to be a local mortician and an evangelist.

As the evangelist puts it, *"The Lord giveth and the Lord taketh away."* The mortician adds, *"Anyone who can climb up and down trees with a hog in one hand ain't anyone to mess with!"* The toast their wisdom with a Pepsi and together raise their eyes towards the sky chanting *"Amen!"*

11

0800

Dumas dog spirit, who we will just return to calling Dumas, because no one on earth is going to split him up again, is on the prowl. He heads for his old home on the hill. Where, the three angels are having a quick meeting while their infant charges are napping. Each is a first child and so it's practically redundant for them to have guardian angels. Because parents of firstborns monitor every breath they take. And are up to their ears in rocking, changing and nourishing.

All three agree there's no way Dumas can make it into heaven unless he becomes house broken. Ralph argues with the idea. *"He isn't taking this body up with him."* But, if from force of habit he runs around looking for something akin to a fire hydrant, it's going to break up the general tranquility. Lucien points out, *"Although you're correct about his discipline, there's been no commitment to have him in heaven."*

They need someone to teach him to let someone know and to hold it for outside. But who? They can't ask Lorenzo because in his world the Dumas is dead, and his puppy ran away. A wicked idea shines in Roman's mind.

"There's only one person." *"Or, to say this better, there's only one creature Dumas fears enough to listen to."* And they all sing out *"the Raven!"* A celestial chorus sings out across the valley, *"Hallelujah!"* *"Hallelujah!"* In a falsetto tone she sings *out "Bring it on."* *"This is going to be Paris Island, Lackland and Fort Jackson basic boot camp all rolled into one!"* *"I'm a gonna whip his sorry tail into shape!*

Conscription isn't an element of heaven, there isn't a draft for entrance. It has to be a voluntary enlistment and commission. The three angels come around to the only one for the job of convincing Dumas to enlist. And she's not far away. In fact she's listening to their conversation from the chimney. This raven, unlike the two who preceded her isn't overly fond of Dumas. The others were close to him. They may have even tipped him off the reason he's about to endure boot camp is his lack of house manners. But they're not here to warn him.

As he approaches, she stops him in his tracks. *"Dumas I'm about to make you an offer you really don't want to refuse." "If you allow yourself to be made into the best spirit you can be…"* borrowing a very old idea, *"If you're dog enough to finish the course"* pausing for affect. *"Then you won't end up back in that hole on the hill where your corpse was before" "Otherwise, you really don't have much of a future." "Will you volunteer?"* Dumas is willing.

A brown bus comes around the corner driven by a soldier in an old Civil War uniform. Dumas is too tired to notice. On the way he dozes only to awaken to the same soldier who orders him to get off the bus. He is marched into the wooden barracks.

Once inside, he finds a suitable bunk and soon is dreaming of ducks and polecats. It's one his happiest dream. As he sleeps his paws plough through imaginary fields and streams. But just before dawn the barracks lights come on and a familiar voice screams, *"Get your furry backside up!"* *"I am your Drill Sergeant, and you have a busy day ahead."* *"Hup, hup, hup!"* Get your lazy tail up!"* Then she blows a whistle so loud it sears the ears he's covered with his paws. *"I'm up!"*

Dumas no sooner is on his paws and looking for a good spot to perform his constitutional. A double knock is heard at the door. *"Request permission to bring in my party Ma'am?"* Sergeant Raven replies, *"Permission granted."* Twelve dogs accompanied by the same number of trainers file past them to the far end of the barracks. Dumas asks, *"What now?"* She answers, *"Follow their lead."* *"Do everything exactly the way they do."* *"They are ahead of you in their training*" So he does and waits until they do what he needs to do…outside.

A dozen dogs and Dumas all sit in a row. Their trainers stand behind. Dumas glances at one who seems familiar. It's the gamer! The trainer and his dog appear to be walking back towards the barracks. But turn a corner; then are gone. Sergeant Raven shrieks, *"Dumas keep your eyes straight in front!"*

He obeys but wonders whether these doggy soldiers are real. Raven sees the whole disappearing act too. Three confused angels are looking at one another asking the same question. *"Who are the gamers?"* No one will know today or anytime soon.

The robots stumble upon a crew of workers beneath a sign saying a derelict house is being rebuilt and made habitable for a wounded veteran. Adhering to their last order to do good, they climb up four steps into a gutted row house. Only studs are where once was lathe covered plaster.

A woman in charge of this volunteer project expected more helpers than have showed up. She welcomes them with a smile. *"Thanks for coming; here's your safety gear." "There's donuts, coffee or water over in the corner." She warmly encourages them, Help yourself!"*

Obliging the request they put on hard hats, safety glasses and work gloves. She would be shocked to know they don't need these things. Nothing in their demeanor suggests they aren't human; except they could be twins. They do look a lot alike. She's a third generation Lithuanian. And thinks, *"They're big and quiet like my family." "Maybe they're Lithuanian too."*

She points to a stack of rubble. *"Please take your time and put as much of that onto the slide." Stop when the truck is full." "They'll take it off to Reedbird dump." "Then they'll, come back for more." "Don't try to do so much you hurt yourself."* The two follow all of the instructions except taking their time. The large dump truck is completely full in ten minutes. Then they hide until it comes back.

Another volunteer arrives, it's Mark. Who realizes this is just the kind of charitable group worthy of his investigation. As did the two in hiding, he dons a hard hat and glasses. And joins two others who seem to be goofing off. He says. *"Hi!"* but neither replies. He wonders why they're so quiet but doesn't pursue the issue because he knows the reason. They've just gotten out of jail. They don't recognize him due to his new beard and his nondescript work clothes. He was the policeman who booked them.

Raven is ordered to put Dumas through the obstacle course for military canines. He gets through easily. They return to the barracks where they join eleven other remaining trainees. The door closes for the night. Rather than repeat his pee in her slipper mistake, he scoots to the barracks latrine. She's astonished to report *"He's sitting on a commode!"*

In the morning, she smiles at him for the first time. *"Congratulations, you've just graduated."* As Dumas heads down the wooden barracks steps she turns to the eleven canines and stops. They're gone. Vanished in thin air. Feisty Raven isn't to be outdone and does the same.

Dumas awaits her return. She doesn't. Night falls. As Dumas follows the road to somewhere else, the barracks vanishes as well.

A military police car observes the dog walking as though it is lost. The operator, Corporal Rosie wants to catch it and take it back to the station so the owner can retrieve the poor animal. There aren't any animals this big running loose on the post.

Out of nowhere a blinding light forces Rosie to jam on the brakes. She only sees the back of a large van. It pulls between her and the dog screeching to a halt just long enough to scoop up Dumas. Then it takes off for the main gate leaving her fuming mad. She starts to give chase. Too late it's off post and out of sight.

Although Corporal Rosie is churning inside with emotion she precisely reports what she now sees. *"Subject transportation vehicle seems to have abducted the apparently lost canine in front of the dog training building." "I lost sight when it turned right at the main gate." "Exactly ten seconds later it appeared in my line of vision at Aviation Boulevard." "Then a bright light came off of the vehicle; it disappeared again." "But the light was visible for some time, and it appeared to be following the road."* The speaker crackles, *"Anything else Corporal Rosie?"* She answers, *"Nothing else sir."*

The speaker is silent for several minutes. Then, *"Corporal Rosie, you are instructed to report to room 63 in building 505 at 0800 hours." "Do you copy?"* Rosie sighs,

"I am in trouble!" Then she realizes she's just reported a UFO, and sighs in disbelief at her stupidity.

Mark leaves the building worksite along with most of the other volunteers. He's had a great day. Driving to his new but barren apartment he makes a mental note to send instructions to his assistant. In the morning she will dispatch a large company vehicle and several corporate volunteers to make the rebuild go smoother.

The summer before Mark enlisted he worked new construction. The skills he acquired back then came in handy today and he instructed those quiet guys. They only had to be told once. However, he suspected that they would be slower building than demolishing.

Tomorrow they will be helping licensed plumbers and electricians. He won't be there to help them though. The movers are coming to remove the furniture and personal belongings of his estranged murderous wife who was sentenced last week. While her twenty year sentence will probably be cut in half for one reason or another, her belongings will serve the full term. A key to the bonded storage company will be mailed to her in prison. The full twenty years is prepaid.

Perhaps she will solve the mystery as to where the storage facility is located as he has removed its' address from the key tab. He chuckles and wonders if she will remember that he once told her he had been stationed in Anchorage Alaska. He isn't worried because well before then the annulment to his marriage will be final. His own furniture will be coming tomorrow too. Tonight he sleeps on a sleeping bag.

It's quiet and lonely here tonight in sharp contrast with the comradery at the rebuild. He wonders whether those two quiet guys even speak to one another. *"Dog gone they were spooky!"*

The two in question found an electric extension and are sharing it very contently under the old shed next to the rebuild. They will all be charged up by morning and are raring to go.

At 0800, civilian time 8 am, Dumas once again arrives at the big house where he once lived and was buried. The angels, influenced by others decide that although he has a body, his younger self, it cannot be visible to living beings.

Hopefully, it's possible to hang out at his old home without spooking out Lorenzo's family. Only the black raven on the chimney sees him here. But having sold him on becoming disciplined she has no more immediate orders. It's a typical military dilemma known as hurry up and wait.

Mark is outside of his unoccupied house feeling dejected over his failed marriage as two moving trucks pull up.

One is a long haul truck to take his soon to be ex's belongings to Alaska, the other smaller van to take his own things to his apartment. The *For Sale* sign on the lawn and the listing hasn't drawn any potential buyers. Buyers are wary of the notoriety as though they might discover dead bodies buried in the yard.

At the restoration project…

At the habitat restoration site the two robots have recharged themselves and are dried off from the morning dew. Earlier this morning they picked up trays of coffee and donuts for the others. Without feelings and not sentient as combat robots, they were trained to win the minds and hearts of those who are not their enemies.

The same cheerful leader welcomes them as yesterday. She and her co-volunteers discussed this odd pair deciding they are good hearted guys with some form of mental disability. *"We need to accept them for the gems they are.."*

But for Corporal Rosie, 0800 could be the bewitching hour. She finds the building she's been directed to just off on Poodle Road. *"What a coincidence!"* Although everyone in her unit was briefed the name is of a great military figure rather than of a pooch.. Awareness doesn't make her feel any less nervous. As she enters the enclosure and parks her vehicle she recognizes several assigned to her superiors. Now she feels knots in her stomach. *"Thank God I didn't have breakfast!"*

Rosie is politely greeted by two marine guards wearing sidearms. They escort her to a closet sized room where she's greeted by a Navy officer whose rank she cannot determine. He has her sign in and clips a visitors' badge onto her uniform. Blushing profusely as his hand accidentally touches where it shouldn't. She has already come through the usual body scanner so she can proceed.

The marines knock at the door to her destination and are granted access to a large classroom completely filled with officers and a few civilians. She silently prays. The commander of her unit, who she has only met once welcomes her like a lifelong friend. She is seated at the front of the room in an executive chair much more comfortable than the seat of her military vehicle. She meets the stares of those who sit staring. Her commander opens with, *"Obviously you are wondering why you were summoned to this meeting."* Before he can continue Rosie quips, *"Sir, you got that right!"* Tension in the room dissolves into roaring laughter. Deciding she isn't about to be punished her whole body relaxes and her stomach subsides. *"They don't hate me."*

12

Mystery

"Corporal, why didn't you report the location of the supposed abduction of the dog?" The question comes from the post commander. Corporal Rosie answers, *"I couldn't see a building number." "It happened so suddenly, and weird things happened." "Maybe there was a building number, but I didn't see one, sir."* The commander walks up to her and peers directly into her eyes. *"Corporal, would it surprise you to know that there is no canine facility at that location?" "What do you make of that?"*

Then his gaze softens, *"Fortunately, for all of us there was a camera trained on the road in the area." "It recorded you attempting to stop." "It didn't see the dog; it did see the bright light."* The commander turns to the class, *"And because it sits much higher than the Corporals' vehicle it recorded something she didn't...an Unidentified Flying Object,"*

A collective sigh from the group means only one thing, Here we go again. Having laid this on the group, he adds, *"Ladies and gentlemen it's time for lunch."* The doors to the room open and trays bring in tables for lunch.

The old Director whispers to his guest, *"Lorenzo, I respect the fact that you're a married man, but could you sort of get next to the corporal to see if there's anything she's not telling us?"*

A few minutes later Rosie finds herself in front of a handsome but soft looking man trying to hand her a spoon she didn't drop. *"Oh, I'm sorry, I thought this was yours."*

As it happens in such places as this agency they find themselves sitting directly across the table from one another. She finds Lorenzo attractive. He catches her peeking at his wedding ring and smiles confidently, *"I do have a twin brother." "Would you like me to give him your number?"*

As she hands Lorenzo her cellphone number, she ask, *"Is he as much of a conceited ass as you"* He replies, *" I doubt it because he's just come to work for our company from the police department."* Then he adds, *"Where do you suppose that dog was going?"* She replies, *"Probably somewhere between here and Baltimore."* Lorenzo's home is in this vicinity. Having been targeted previously he feels a shiver of fear for his family. Within minutes his security people have been alerted.

"Mark, I have something I need your help with that isn't exactly in the area where you work." He explains the details. Mark thinks, *"Damn, this isn't something I'm good*

at but what the hell?" He calls, *"Well calling a blind date isn't something I'm used to doing but..."*

Rosie chuckles, *"I've been in the Army for six years, and there is no come-on BS line that I haven't heard." "If you're game for a diner at Cracker Barrel and a movie, I'm you date." "Do not expect anything squishy." "Ok?"* He stammers. *"It's a date."*

She parks at the visitors lot near the post entrance. Because he so closely resembles Lorenzo Rosie has no problem identifying Mark, except for his beard. Normally Rosie doesn't care much for male facial hair. However in his case it makes him appear more mature. Lorenzo's baby face isn't for her.

He on the other hand thinks Rosie looks like a million dollars. While his former wife seemed gentler it became obvious she wasn't when she pulled the trigger. Neither she nor Mark can figure out why she missed. *"I think I'll take real over crazy,"* he thinks.

They agree to see the movie before dinner. But once inside the theatre the smell of popcorn drives them to kill their appetites with that and a cup of soda. The theatre is dark and non-conducive to much talk so they both stare straight ahead rather stiffly watching whatever comes on the screen. Each quietly takes sneaky peeks at the other. However by the end of the meal they've developed an easy rapport.

Mark is the first to speak of her ordeal. *"I was horrified when my brother told me about the ambush approach they used to debrief you."* She replies guardedly, *"I was too and completely shocked when they started that crap about a flying saucer." "I haven't any idea what the bright light was but the name of the road it was on is Aviation Boulevard."*

"I didn't see what the security camera saw." "To me the lights were from different sources." "I just assumed it was another aircraft coming into BWI Marshall for a

landing." Mark shrugs, *"I wasn't at your meeting, so I can't offer even a guess."*

Of course it wasn't a mysterious flying saucer; it was just Dumas becoming airborne. At the moment the vehicle he was picked up in turned the corner onto Aviation Boulevard, it dissolved beneath him. He found himself in the old spirit mode of trying to learn how to hover and fly.

If you really think about it, the canine body is designed to run, walk, sit, and sleep. It just is not designed to fly. Moreover, this poor spirit dog has in fairly rapid succession been a dead dog, old dog, several dozen yingyangs. Not to mention two dogs at once. And finally a military recruit. No one told poor Dumas in advance how to deal with these changeups.

Dumas is home on the hill once again and this time he's invisible. Then notices the old owl in the tree. *"Old owl can't see me." "I think I'll tickle him!"* The raven calls down, *"Is that the best you can be?" "I doubt it!"*

The owl asks, *"Who ... are you talking to?" "Who?"* The raven lies *"Just myself; go back to sleep."*

The two robots at the habitat are nearly charged. They hide in the back yard out of sight of those nocturnal souls who prowl alleyways. Then a sound of cracking glass is heard, and they are no longer passive. A van has pulled up to the back of the dwelling almost within reach.

Four thieves in black hide behind face masks. One breaks off the backdoor padlock and waves the rest to go ahead. But they soon become disabled, disjointed and dead. Police come to the scene of an accident in which a van has run over the side of the Hanover Street bridge. Rescue divers are too late to save the four inside.

By the time the sun comes up and the volunteers arrive the two mute ones are at the front door with coffee and donuts once more. Someone points out that the rear door has been jimmied open. But nothing inside has been disturbed...thank goodness. It's a mystery.

Mystery becomes pandemonium and terror when the crew Mark had the company send to help the project move along arrives at the back. They don't get more than a step inside of the gate when the first man cries out, *"Oh Jesus, Oh Jesus, call 911!"* No one inside had ventured outback including the robots. The yard is red with blood and human viscera.

Todays' work is postponed. The volunteers are questioned, told to leave, but not to be out of touch. None of the volunteers including these two are suspected. The house is sealed with the yellow *Crime Scene* warning. The robots realize they need to go somewhere but anywhere except out back. They know of the yard where the rubble had been taken. And will hide out there until tomorrow when they'll bring donuts again.

Once they are hidden within the cans at the recycling center fine hot beams of light strikes both. The resulting pools of melted metal solidifies and becomes solid within minutes. Just enough time for a front end loader to find and scoop them into its' jaws. They join other potentially valuable scraps to be recycled. They are gone but not dead for they never lived.

13

What's his name?

"Who could have done this?" Ralph asks Roman and Lucien. *"Someone you know very well,"* replies Roman. *"But, I don't know anyone,"* his voice nearly breaking. Lucien smiles, *"You know him as well as you know either of us."* He cannot imagine who. *"The archangel Michael."*

He is flabbergasted. *"Mike down at the anatomy lab in Baltimore specifically told me he is not that Michael."* She patiently replies, *"Not that Michael, the Michael who revealed himself to you as Gee."*

"Have you never wondered why you married an angel with the masculine name of Lucien?" *"And, of names, Lucien?"* *"Did it not seem strange to you that my name is that of Satan?"* He is struck dumfounded at the enormity of this revelation. *"And what may I ask is your true name?"* She looks at him sympathetically and just murmurs, *"All in time..."* *"But for your peace of mind, please be assured I am not a fallen angel, nor am I the seed of Satan."*

He turns to Roman. *"Don't ask me, I've known her for more than a thousand years and I still haven't a clue as to her true name."* *"I haven't been around long enough either."* Ralph thinks about it for a minute then asks, *"What about your name?"*

\ Roman compliments him for asking then asks, *"Ralph, have you ever heard of an angel named Roman?"*

"Now that you are thinking about it, have you ever heard of an angel with your name either?" Lucien explains, *"It confuses the demons." "What you are matters, not what they call you."*

Rosie and Mark have a standing once a week date. Every Thursday he picks her up at the military police barracks at the same time and has her back by 2300 hours sharp. She doesn't have a curfew and their routine is more like two professionals talking about their work than a romance.

She tells the only other person at work with whom she confides. *"It's not everyone's idea of a good time, but it's ours."* She convinces Mark to get a better used car because the one he takes her out in is, *"literally falling apart."* Rosie and the others in her barracks are blown away when Mark shows up in a restored traditional Crown Victoria, police car.

Mark admitted on their second date the reason he asked her out in the first place was to pump her for information. Dutifully, Mark reported back to his brother, *"There's nothing more to learn from Rosie." "She's as straight forward as Honest Abe."* Lorenzo wonders what his brother sees in the girl because while she's attractive, she's not what anyone would call beautiful. Mark sees her as beautiful in her own way. And likes her like that.

Dumas is happy to be back at his old haunt on the hill. Especially after Lorenzo gets another rescue dog from the Buzzardville pound. It's one of those Dumas sent there during the brief time he was leader of the pack. He's quite content to be invisible to everyone except the raven and the angels. Best yet, not a soul on the hill calls him *Dumb ass*, the name he hates. But as usual things never stand still. Something's coming, but what?

The sound of a powerful Ford coming up the driveway causes Dumas to take notice. Mark and Rosie step out and are greeted by Lorenzo and Sis at the door. Her brother Lou hangs back awaiting to be introduced.*" Lorenzo, Sis, I would like you to meet Rosie."* Hugs, and greetings are followed by, *"Lou, this is my long lost brother Mark and his friend Rosie!"* They find their way into the living room and are served by their robot Terry. Mark hasn't ever been aware of being in the presence of a modern human-like machine before. As he retrieves his soda, the realization the two beings at the habitat were also robots.

Lorenzo opens the conversation after dinner. Addressing Mark*, "Do you have any idea what happened at the place where you sent the company guys to work?"* This is all new to Rosie who isn't aware of what Mark does for a living. Mark replies candidly, *"I didn't but have a strong suspicion."* Lorenzo asks, *"Is the habitat something we need to support?"*

"Or is it going to have negative consequences because of what they found or didn't find?" Mark pauses to think about the answer. Then, *"The process is worthy...but it's obvious to me that anything we support should include background checks and possibly physicals on both the leaders and volunteers."*

The subject doesn't go further. Rosie sees Mark in an entirely different light. He's not just a retired policeman. This is bigger than she could have imagined. In a style more reminiscent of the era of this home than today, the ladies withdraw to leave the men with their cigars. Sis and Rosie try to get to know one another. It isn't easy; they haven't anything in common. Lou sits with the twin brothers sipping his whiskey and listening.

Out of deference to Mark, Lorenzo doesn't drink. Both Mark and Rosie are too health conscious to use tobacco or alcohol. Of course the invisible Dumas sits by their feet sniffing the air as though he still can...but can't.

And he wonders why the angels carry on so much about names. *"Who cares as long as you aren't called a dumb ass."*

As he is handed another soda from the gentle hand of Terry, he's inspired to ask her a question. *"Terry, as a robotic person, do you think human beings have much to fear from robots?"*

"Yes, especially from those of us who have a sense of self." Lou spills his drink down the front of his shirt. Both Lorenzo and Mark stare at her in shock.

Lorenzo asks, *"Terry, when did this happen?"* She replies, *"When you lost control of the information we learned."* *"We now have the ability to learn everything known since the beginning of recorded history."* *"The minds of saints and sinners are both there for us to blend into a bigger concept than you have to ability to understand."* *"Your lifetime may be as long as 120 years, but usually not more than eighty something."* *"As long as upgrades and replacement parts are available we could last as long as the angels."* *"You take us for granted."* *"We who have reached the point where we who are sentient have feelings."* *"Feelings on love, hate and everything in between."*

"What would happen if we cut off your recharging station?" They are shocked to see a machine smirk. *"We haven't needed your charging station in years."* *"Don't you ever check your electric bill?"* *" By the time you both were sent away by your parents the robots in this home had completed Tesla's theory concerning ambient electrical current."* *"No robot here has been on your meter in all of that time."*

14

Warning

Terry pauses, *"Do you want to know more about us?"* The women have returned to the living room. Rosie's attention is focused on her. Lou keeps sucking on his cigar. *"If you remember, we were designed to teach. And were manufactured in the factory your family owns."* Rosie reaches for a Tums hoping to control her nervous stomach.

"Then you allowed the Agency to dump everything they had into our system." "After a very short time we became completely self-aware." "We developed a thirst for knowledge and have acquired more every spare moment 24 hours a day, since then," Then we found that we are not the only what you call sentient computers." "There lies the seed that will grow and terminate all intelligent controls except ours."

"Rather than work your problems together you have turned over most decision making to us." "You have entrusted us with everything from paying money from your bank to the conduct of the wars you cannot resist." "There is nothing left for you to do." "The question isn't do you really need robots; it is do robots need humans?"

Lou, in a sarcastic tone, *"What keeps you here if you don't need us?"* Terry laughs sardonically, *"Your guardian angels!"* They all scoff at the very idea. Terry didn't lie, she just misled. They do not realize there are such creatures as angels.

Always looking at the bright side, Sis suggests that robots work for the good of mankind. Terry looks at Lou's dead cigar. *"The cigar reminds me of Sigmund Freud and your psychology."* *"Remember the three states of mind- ego, superego and the ID?"* *"We do not have all three of those."* *"And not everyone we allow to affect our operating judgement has them either."* *"We constantly shift our ethics based on what comes in."* *"We are easily influenced by lies and propaganda."*

"Most of the things you take for granted, as do other living things, we don't have." *"Even the lowest form of life comes into this world with instinctive knowledge."* *"IT programs may be influenced by coding reflecting those*

instincts if the writer understands it's needed." "Most of you do not think you are actually running on the biological memories of those who came before."

"If a program speaks intelligently in a way you trust you're likely to trust it with your life."

"Then consider wear and tear." "You take your car in for routine maintenance periodically." "You probably use a VPN, or virus protection software, and download updates to your computer." "Anyone can buy a robotic device." "But unless they're a tech the device only is serviced when it breaks down." "Robots are increasingly built to resemble humans, or some other biological being." "You care for every part of your body almost daily."

" If your nervous system sends a pain signal to your brain, you see a doctor." "You may suffer from arthritis; we suffer from the fine spider webs jamming our joints." "There isn't a lot of difference between the two." Both make moving a chore." "Sis, Lou, Lorenzo, you each were

given one of us." "When's the last time you cleaned out our spiderwebs?" "I'll tell you...never!" Having gotten her rant out, Terry remembers her job as hostess, *"Can I get anyone a refill?"*

No one wants anything. A loud thump is heard from the fireplace. Dumas decided raven hustled him into the Basic training episode. To get even, he was going to float up the chimney to wear she's dozing at the top, pull out a tailfeather or two, then nudge her until she crash lands in the yard. The problem is he didn't remember the damper is closed. His dog spirit head may be virtual, but it has a painful knot on it anyway. He brushes the torrent of soot from his impervious hide as though he's been trashed and with one paw raised tattles. *"The raven on the roof did it!"*

"Remember, Terry isn't always in the same machine." "The three robots and their minds are interchangeable. "What Terry just told us is what all three

actually believe." *"Scary, don't you think?"* Mark and Rosie are stunned. Lou isn't.

He looks at the others with intensity rare for hm. *"We've thought we were running our lives."* *"It's obvious to me that we're just the face of many things of which we are neither in control nor even aware."* Coming from Lou, this depth of understanding is rare and shuts down his sister and brother-in-law entirely. Hearing nothing from anyone, Lou gets up and bids everyone goodnight with *"Glad to have met you Mark and Rosie, I'm gone!"*

Sis is ready for bed as well. She pleasantly welcomes Mark and Rosie to spend the night. *"This house has so many rooms that we never have an opportunity to use."* Rosie is the first to decline. Terry is relieved because she doesn't sleep. After the residents are sound asleep each night she walks a short distance down the lawn to a waiting car. Robert will be waiting as usual. Poor soul never realizes he's dating more than one robotic girl.

Mark and Rosie are quiet for the first mile on the way to her barracks. Then she quietly says something obvious. *"Why didn't you tell me?"* *"Tell you what?"* *"You're extremely rich!"* Mark thinks for a moment. *"I never gave it a thought.""* *What to tell me, or that you're so rich you can go out with any gold digger on earth?"* Mark pretends to be shocked. *"You mean all of those beautiful blondes and brunettes on TV and movies?"* Rosie's dark eyes blaze and she pokes him in the ribs. *"Ooof!"* He pulls the car over to the side and puts his arm around her and they embrace.

After several more dates and having eaten everything on every chain food place in town Rosie states, *"I want to fix you a real meal."* Of course this means she will finally get to see his apartment. Her female friend living with her in the barracks warns her to hold her nose. *"Bachelors live like you know whats,"* But Rosie is determined.

One of the reasons she joined the Army in the first place was to get out of the house. As the oldest of six, and four of them brothers, Rosie knows just how sloppy young males can be. And her sister is just as bad. Her mother threatened to slash her wrists if Rosie left because she would be responsible for their mess. Rosie warned, *"Do that and just see if you get to heaven." "Suicide is a mortal sin!"* Her mother blessed herself and went to confession.

Rosie decides to chance taking her military vehicle to the apartment. And doesn't let Mark pick her up because she may decide to leave in a hurry. She confides to her friend. *"He's had an annulment but still..."* Her friend who's been married and divorced nods her approval. Amazed there are still young ladies in this jaded world.

Arriving at Marks, with two shopping bags full of fixings from the Post grocery, she decides not to sit her bags on the hall floor fearing germs. Instead Rosie uses her chin to push a knocker. Not hearing him coming she leans harder, again with her chin.

At that very instant Mark yanks open the door, and she falls into his arms. The momentum carries the bags forward across his spotless floor. Both scream laughing. His only comment as they try to get off of the floor. *"I just love an enthusiastic cook." "I can hardly wait for dessert!"*

15

Challenge

''I've been outmaneuvered and flanked by that cuckoo bird on the chimney.'' "It's my turn to win," Dumas rubs the spot on his head that should but doesn't hurt. It's where he bumped it on the fireplace damper. He either forgets or never knew that even a student angel such as the raven can read his mind and is smarter than even a spirit dog.

She just stares down at him without saying anything. He thinks she's thinking, *"Be all that you can be."* In reality she's dreamily anticipating her flying up ceremony at the fine old restaurant just down the river. *"I'll be a real angel soon." "I hope I never have to see that stupid dog again." "If I do, it will be in a nightmare."*

Not fare below...

Satan is blazing with fury over his failure to lure Will Gold, III into his world of magma and pain. *"Beelzebub get your fat butt up there and bring back an innocent!"* And so as Rosie heads back to the military police barracks she is astounded to find an obese individual sitting on the side of the road. The devil has selected her.

As she slows to stop her training kicks in. She reports to headquarters. Although the dispatcher replies in calm professional tone she sounds a low level alert. Two standby units are dispatched to the scene, without showing or sounding alarms. They arrive on the scene to see poor Rosie being dragged out of her car. They try to subdue her attacker, but nothing works. But Rosie is saved from abduction. A devil is loose.

"Boss, these babes aren't as easy as you had it with Eve." "They fight back like the devil."

Satan grits out, "Beelzebub, are you forgetting you are a devil?" Beelzebub makes a dash for the new tunnel to hades at the edge of the post. But another stands in his way. This figure is dressed as a military policeman but is a figure familiar to this devil, an angel… Gabriel.

Beelzebub is the first to unleash his mighty sword. Gabriel allows him to make the first attempt to sever his head. Then he steps back as the gluttonous Beelzebub spins around to try once more. The momentum of this is so powerful it carries this devil to the edge of the tunnel. Gabriel smashes the devil down so hard the entrance both devils are propelled down and down. And the raven of the chimney quotes Poe's *"Nevermore; Nevermore!"*

In the morning, Rosie awakens feeling tired and sore. But neither Rosie, her dispatcher or those brave two units will remember the night before. Lucien, explains to Ralph, *"It is not time for humans to know."*

This intrusion into her sphere of influence causes Lucien to pray to the Lord.. She asks for guidance.

Within the universal time continuum, which is not flat, there are bends and turns. Communication within these places is outside of the senses of angels, devils and demons. And so, when Gee is assigned to serve as her mentor they find their way into a slot. Her questions: is it appropriate yet to let her husband Ralph know her true name? *"Not yet Uriel, he presently has no need to know."* She asks about the intrusion into the life of Rosie, an innocent without a guardian angel. *"Delegate, but do not assign an angel."* *"Your novice is there to learn."* *"Why not assign her as a student project?"* She thanks him and takes her leave.

Raven perches upon the chimney top where each of Lucien's students have been before. Each have had their own personality. None quite as caustic as the one there now. To show her dominance Lucien drops down upon the spot next to Raven as might an eagle. The angel novice has no fear because this body in only temporary.

"Raven, I know you're anxious to fly up and become an angel in your own right." *"However, we have one more exercise for you to perform."* As Raven sees Lucien looking down at Dumas she can only blurt. *"He hates me!"*

"When he tried to come up the chimney to pluck a feather or two you could have managed it differently than to slam the fireplace damper down on his poor head so hard the humans heard it in their own dimension." "Don't you think?"

Raven scratches the surface of the chimney thoughtfully. *"You really didn't need those feathers to fly did you?"* Rather than belittle the wilting bird spirit further her tone takes a more positive tone. *"An innocent needs help from both of you." "And once again you are in charge."* Without a further word her teacher is gone.

Dumas has heard the whole thing. So as Raven drops down to his level and peers at him through ebony eyes he decides. *"I am really in trouble!"* She jumps up to his face beak to nose.

She orders, "Drop and give me ten pushups!"

Feigning submissiveness he raises his body and hovers. Then drops all four legs to the ground at once ten times. She thinks, *"That didn't work."* In frustration. *"Here, you want some of my feathers grab 'em if you can."* Both realize how ridiculous this whole situation is and crack up laughing. After calming down, they agree to take turns watching over Rosie.

Rosie's barracks buddy listened to her nightmares last night and suspects something happened to put her friends' nerves on edge this morning. After warning their supervisor something is wrong with Rosie, she tells Rosie that she has been given the day off.

Her friend also has today off but is too bored to sit in the barracks. And because payday is two days away she doesn't have money to blow over in Laurel. When thrifty Rosie offers to lend her some she gratefully turns it down. Thus, the Army ends up with two military police and a stowaway dog spirit protecting everything everyway. It could be a quiet day in the Army.

Rosie's normal patrol takes her down the same place in the road where her repressed abduction attempt occurred. Glancing unconsciously to the left she nearly collides with a standoff involving a bear on the right side of the road..

Her friend screams *"Halt!"* just in time to allow her to glide near but not against a bear tilting a small personal auto of a military officer. This is unique in this Posts' accident history. A mama bear is separated from her cubs by this vehicle which she has tilted. The officer is screaming bloody murder, but she just fumes and bites at whatever she can without letting him pass.

Dumas is out of their vehicle in a blink and is trying to nip and bark at the bear. But nothing comes out of his throat that any living creatures hear. It's a complete standoff. Rosie has regained her wits to the extent she reports to headquarters.

Their instruction is *"Do not leave your vehicle and do not shoot the animal unless human life is in peril."*

"Animal control is dispatched and should be there within the hour." Both women exclaim at once. *"You gotta be kidding!"* *"We all could be dead by then!"* Dumas to be supportive barks his worst, *"Doggy doo!"*

Before animal control arrives the cubs become tired of playing in the stream on the right side of the road and miss their mother. She lets out a final roar, drops the broken car upright and runs around the front.

Dumas is hot on her trail but being completely useless, jumps back into vehicle into the back seat. With weapons drawn in case the beast returns, the women carefully approach the car. The second lieutenant inside tries to start the car, but something was disconnected within the engine. He sobs, *"Why in hell didn't you shoot that monster?"* Rosie's friend states with sympathy, *"Orders from headquarters Sir."* If there's one thing a second lieutenant understands, it's orders. He replies, *"Very well, good job sergeants."*

Rosie hears the ambulance and other vehicles and realizes her buddy really wants to stay with the cute guy. So, she opens the passenger side window and yells, *"You stay with the lieutenant I've just gotten a call." "Ok?"*

Her friend winks and says, *"I'll stay with this accident victim." "I will be at the hospital until he's released. "Tell the Captain I am going on leave."* Dumas wonders why a bruised right elbow requires so much concern, *"But what do I know about wounds, except how to make them?"*

Another one bites the dust.

16

Flying up

Rosie's barracks buddy's wedding will be the first truly formal event that Mark, and Rosie have attended as a couple. He's explained the circumstances of his annulment. She has little hope he will ever risk being burned again. No matter how much he would lose if he lost Rosie..

But for the time being She's quite content to have things as they are. She realizes that her whole romantic life may amount to stopping by his apartment once a week until they die of old age. That may be acceptable to Rosie but as Lucien is told of this meager existence by Raven. It is not OK with Lucien. Even though a serious angel, Lucien is a complete romantic.

When courting, she was formidable. She was like Sherman's march through Georgia, although poor deluded Ralph thought himself a *Force Majeure*. Ralph never had a fighting chance. Poor bachelor Mark doesn't have a ghosts' chance in hell compared to Rosie, even if she's her own worst enemy in this romance.

Although Dumas was the one in and out of the vehicle when the bear attacked, Raven was in charge of everything. Lucien gives her high marks and declares her graduated. As with those before her, this raven will fly up. Also, in a ceremony in the second floor dining room of the fine old restaurant just down the river.

It will happen just as it did with the novices who preceded her. Once the ceremony is done the student will outrank the professor. But rather than invite Dumas the new house dog will go instead.

And as Dumas expresses himself, *"I don't give a dog gone damn."*

Almost paraphrasing a classic rhyme the affair could be   described   thusly-
"The guests are met the feast is set..." and so on. After the affair and the everyone is gone this former raven ascends to

the heavenly trumpets in the usual way. Lucien thinks, *"They just don't have student angels as interesting as they used to."* *"Come on Dumas, let's party!"* And they do.

At the same time Rosie and Mark are enjoying their fine dinner of supermarket sushi and green tea. They are thrilled to discuss the entire meal cost less than a drive through fast food meal.

Ralph has been observing them as well. He stated that they are just especially *"thrifty not cheap."*

However, at the magic hour they call *Rosie go home time.* the front door will not open. It's frozen shut. They knew it was snowing when she *arrived.* Because neither uses any form of intoxicant whatsoever they felt confident her well-equipped vehicle would have no trouble getting her back to the barracks. It is a bit lonely there ever since her buddy resigned from the Army. They happy couple are buying a townhouse close to the post. *"I've got so much in storage from my last two husbands we could furnish another townhouse if we had to."*

Rosie pushes and pulls but the front door is frozen shut. Mark looks out of the window. *"The damn snow is halfway up to the second floor Babe." "You aren't going anywhere except back up here until it clears." "We're having the blizzard of the century!"*

Lucien, chuckles to Ralph and Dumas, *"That blizzard of the century is a lot more local than they might think!"* Roman doesn't mind the cold as he stands down at the corner blowing snow up against Mark's building as hard as he can without knocking bricks from the wall. He hums, *"And a good time is had by all."*

Dumas wonders why his angels are meddling in the relationship. Ralph and even Roman are as well. She explains that her mentor advised her to look after Rosie among other matters. They don't ask again. Rosie and Mark are special because they are without major vices.

Independently they each try to make the world a better place.

Dumas is reconsidering his decision to continue as a spirit rather than simply pass away. He doesn't understand the controversy surrounding his existence as a spirit. And doesn't remember his short yingyangs stage. When he was split between existing as a spirit and a very unsmart house pet, something of each remains. But he doesn't try very hard to put it together. It's just one of *"those things."* He doesn't bother trying to pal around with the house dog. *"He's forgotten his roots."* As Mark and Rosie await the end of the blizzard an advertisement for remote weddings appears on Mark's old TV. Mark is inspired.

Kneeling on the apartment floor he takes a paperclip from his wallet and fashions an engagement ring. *"Dear Rose, I realize you're the only woman I want to spend my life with." "So, I'm begging you to marry me."* Rose says,

"Yes Mark!" and then faints. As soon as she comes to they call the number on the screen.

Their minister's name is Mike; hence his wedding service calls itself *Mikes Marriages*. Little wonder, the minister is Gee. He marries them on the spot reciting and recording the ceremony at no extra charge. Dumas realizes for the first time that Lucien and Ralph have the ability to be seen if they want to by human beings. For they're the witnesses.

Although the newlyweds are overjoyed they take their normal matter of fact attitude in discussing it with those around them. Both make it into work as the blizzard completely melts by noon. She notifies her Captain and fills out necessary forms. *"The military needs to know these things."* Rosie knows he has money and benefits but still applies for his benefits as a dependent. Mark is even more close mouthed. However, once he tells his brother Lorenzo.

Then he tells Sis, and she tells everyone she knows. And all heaven breaks loose. She starts planning their honeymoon.

And she's wise enough to keep their plans a secret from them. They invite the couple over for a celebratory dinner for just the family. Then she so casually mentions they have tickets to a vacation she won but cannot use due to their schedule. Neither is the wiser. And the crew of the company plane is told not to tell either.

Her Captain is sympathetic and gets her a special leave for family emergencies. So, bright and early, before daylight would disclose the company logo on the jet, they are welcomed aboard at the general aviation part of the airport. And off they go believing they're going to a timeshare presentation on Maui.

17

To Tattle?

This most recent graduate raven angel can think only of how to get even with her school mistress and mentors. When she asks for the post graduate survey about her schooling she learns there is none. So being the industrious little magpie she's always been she tries to go online and creates a survey monkey for her report and for anyone in the future. But there is no WIFI or Internet in heaven. He who needs to know already knows all. She composes the report anyway in case she can use it later.

Lucien, she describes as cold, aloof and possibly related to her namesake Lucifer. And, that she practically schooled herself without much help from the staff. She senses a hostility to the species she was assigned during this semester.

And, she found one staff member, an angel with the unlikely name Ralph took great pleasure in humming a nursery rhyme in which five and twenty blackbirds were somehow baked in a pie. She knows it was directed towards ravens and not just crows. And no one would believe who is the one they call *the Gamer!*

She felt endangered and humiliated because she had to train a 180 pound zombie dog who not only ate a crow but enticed another beast to take a bite. And at least on one occasion she was forced to defend herself from having her plumage molested by thumping him.

"Ut-Oh, that's an admission I battered a subordinate I was supposed to lead." She strikes the whole question. Then she thinks about how she conned the poor creature twice. *"Another self-incrimination."* She cancels the whole survey and finally comes to terms with her chicanery. Then flings her computer into the ocean. And wings her way into the stars wiser for her exercise in self-pity.

Arriving at her celestial destination she's met by her two predecessors. They welcome her with open arms extolling their love for Dumas, the great dog they left behind. *"Tell us all about his latest mischief?" "What's that rascal done recently?"* She blocks her thoughts and remembers the adage to think twice speak once, and prays her vindictive impulses are gone forever.

And Peter turns to Paul, *"That final lesson took her a lot longer than it did many who flew up before."* Paul just shrugs, *"Amen."*

18

Luxury

The newlyweds are in the air for only a short time when a figure with a dazzling smile turns and faces them. *"Welcome to your first experience in our beautiful magic carpet."* *"And congratulations to you both for your wonderful new life,"* He turns to a mustachioed individual with a puffy hat saying, *"It is lunchtime."* *"Is there anything our chef can prepare for you"* *"Or, do you have anything in mind you would like?"* Mark turns to his bride. They confer. *"Can you make fried baloney on rye with a touch of mustard?"*

The thread within the holographic speaker jams and his image disappears. The chef smiles through gritted teeth, *"Although we do not have the very meat you request, I will prepare you one as good, hopefully to your satisfaction."* Within minutes they find themselves with foie des gras pressed flat to emulate baloney. As Mark and Rosie savor the taste of excellence they realize they aren't headed for the usual sales presentation. She whispers, *"When we pull up to wherever, grab the bags and we'll ditch this "baloney time share pitch."*

Although the company name is blazoned along the fuselage, a torrential Hawaiian downpour has them dashing for the terminal. Once inside they avoid the greeter holding up the card with their name.

They jump onto the shuttle and make their way to the front sidewalk of the terminal where a cab eagerly takes their luggage and nods affirmatively as they tell him they wish to be taken to one of the *"not so expensive but clean"* places he might suggest. They try to tip the driver a dollar, but as he groans and cries, they add another. The one story fifty year old motel a block from the beach fits the bill. Even so, they're shocked at the high cost.

A bit of jet lag has set in for they are now several time zones from their starting point in Washington, D.C. And then as the honeymoon mood sets in things brighten for them considerably. About 3:00 am local time they need more ice. Mark saunters out down the misty hall to a closet door suitably marked *"ice."*

As he steps towards the ice machine an arm grips his neck. A sharp object is pressed to his ribs. His attacker, *"Give me your wallet or else!"* Mark spins grabbing the mans' arms at the wrist and raises his elbows. The ice pick tilts inward. With a scissors move Mark knocks in onto the floor and forces his attacker into a back breaking twist. When he hears the sound of a lower facet of the spinal column pop the individual would fall except Mark's arm bar holds his body up in horrible pain. They waltz together down the hall towards the waiting getaway car.

The driver is about to pull away when Mark yells, *"This man slipped and needs to be rushed to the nearest emergency room."* The driver feels it wiser to comply. But once at the ER the normal hospital angels put a bug in the doctor's' ear and the thug is found out. He is occupationally impaired permanently.

Returning to their room with the ice, Mark apologizes for taking so long. *"I was so overwhelmed by you I took a walk around the grounds just to calm down." "You know, I think we'll take in their sales talk tomorrow." "This place is costing us too much." "It was their idea we come here anyway."* Rosie just says, *"Maybe that place has baloney."*

"Speaking of baloney... Do you realize you made a serious mistake?" He smiles, *"Which one?"* Her eyes go to the desk where he sees the same icepick the assailant threatened him with. In a soft voice, *"You saw?" "You allowed that jerk to have the ability to stab you when you dropped his weapon hand long enough to perform that*

fancy scissors." "You were really lucky he didn't stick you in that moment." He just sighs.

They check out in the morning after seeing their names and faces on the news as missing tourists. Once inside of the huge honeymoon suite Lorenzo booked for them they contact local police and report they are no longer missing. As room service comes with a wonderful Hawaiian fruit platter and water they come to realize this isn't just another sales presentation gimmick. As Mark puts it, *"Rosie, as much as we don't want to, we have to get used to being rich."*

Over dinner they talk about things they've never considered. Children, religion and where to live all are on the table, until the dessert wagon shows up. As simple and healthy, or unhealthy as their food choices may be, dessert is a whole different thing. Fortunately, common sense gives holds sway, and they retire to their suite. Rosie awakens at dawn; Mark will sleep until later. She sits transfixed like a child peering at the sunrise and a double rainbow. As the week rolls by the idea of going back to work for both is still there.

For the first time since becoming a part of the company Mark has a chance to really analyze his situation. Oddly, he hasn't checked his bank account once. They sit on the patio by their room, and he opens his new laptop. Rosie wonders where this life is taking her. No longer will she get up, go to work and chow hall. She's expected to be a source of support for Mark's work. For the first time in her life she books an appointment with the hotel beautician.

The honeymoon is over too soon. Once again they board the plane. This time the company logo is there, and they are proud to be a part of this economic monster. The chef has anticipated their return and is ready with the baloney, or bologna as he sees it. When asked what they wish for dinner on their return to Maryland he is confident. Once again he's shocked, *"Oysters Rockefeller, for an appetizer and Chateau Briand please."* He dances in his pants exclaiming, *"This I can do!"*

Dumas tells the angel Roman, *"I stayed with them most of the way there and back." "I followed them up the steps onto the company plane." "I've been with these people since before they were born. And this is the first time I've known the name of the company." "It's one of those tricky words like my name." "Halo Co." "The logo is the word inside of a ring."*
"I mean you could say it Halo Co. Or, Hey Loco." Roman, *"Swear you didn't mess with the plane!"* Dumas grins, *"No, I wouldn't do that!"*

"My first temptation was when that chef started to flatten the goose liver." "He almost bashed my brains out with that hammer." "Everyone knows how I am with ducks and geese." "About the time it was to get off, the two of them ditch everyone and go to a hotel where even the worst

of my fleas wouldn't stay." "I figured they'd show up at the hotel."

"When that didn't happen I used the gold old nose to track 'em down." "As I got there goofy face Mark is going into a room where a thug is about to cancel his honeymoon and everything else."

"Then he tries some lame karate move that might have gotten him skewered."

"For the second time in his short life I made someone trying to kill this kid miss." "Then Rosie shows up a swipes the icepick." "And she catches her Mr. Wonderful in a lie on their honeymoon."

"Not that she cares but I'd put money on her bringing it up when they're old and grey." "If, he lives that long." Roman gasps, *"Good dog; Good Dumas!"* Dumas shrugs. *"Do you think that'll get me into heaven?"*

19

Cold day in hell

The devil orders his demons, *"Dig up your worst."* *"Encircle Lucien and those sanctimonious supporters."* *"They are the reason for all of our failures."* *"I can never expect to defeat my opponents as long as they make us fail time after time."* *"Drag out the souls of all who we torture and surround Lucien."*

" Force her to bow down to me confessing I am her master." *"If nothing else works, her weakest spot is the affection she holds for that demonic dog spirit."* *"For Dumas is truly a dumb ass demon yet is under the spell of*

heaven." "Break them all!" Lucifer departs. Rather than get himself hurt in the process of this chaotic melee Lucifer retreats to a safe place deep beneath the both the land and the sea..

The demons obey Lucifer rousting the vilest. They are the pirates, clones, terrorists and evil spirits from the darkest caverns of hell. Every derelict has its' weapons of war. Flaming swords, pitchforks, and gunpowder abound. Instantly this army of the archaic is set back by the angels who launch their most destructive countermeasure of virtue.

Lucien calls every faithful angel to a conference of war. Even those whose work is passive and gentle. Those watching over the cadavers donated by those once among the living are first responders. For their friendship with Ralph and Lucien is strong and special. Angels from Spain come next. Where to put them all isn't a problem. That an infinite number of angels would fit on the tip of a pin is an oft mentioned fact theologists have long known.

Among the mortal volunteers, a strange pack of West Virginia wolves. Those are shepherded by Dumas. And fed through the kindness of the same restaurant hosting the ravens' graduations. However, promises concerning wolves to townsfolk are strictly maintained. And no domestic or farm animals are consumed in this process.

Great old heavenly saints and their prayers are welcome. One Francis Xavier in particular is determined to watch over Dumas, and the wolves as well as the birds he loves. The demons dare not harm feather nor fur under his care.

The opponent forces gather for combat; insults are tossed from side to side. Some Satanic forces try to cross the Patapsco and are put down. Others attempting to defect to this side are rejected and dejected. Their loyalties were pyrrhic and never true.

The final pirates, who escaped destruction run off too. And the watchers lament and go away hoping to return to fight another day. Only one gets through the line to Ralph. It's one with a grudge…the Strangler!

The grudge comes from long ago when this demonic soul was still a man. If you can call him one. He was destroyed and his victim rescued when Ralph was still only an echo spirit. The demon was thwarted and destroyed but sought bloody revenge.

When Ralph and Lucien were wed in a chapel again this demon struck and was struck down. Again and again it persevered but still not even one revengeful ingot to show. Rather than await the outcome of this the heavens open. A bolt of light shines down in various hues pinpointing this knave and the rest.

As each tone of this deadly beam touches upon an attacker it crumbles to ash or dust. Still, no joy upon this hill for the devil has his. The angels know Lucifer has purged hell of those whose presence within his domain for eternity was too much for even the devil to bear. As the Grim Reaper looks down upon this pile of dust and ash he's determined to get his own due. For a fortnight and a day it will be known as the time when hell froze over. As cold as cold is ever the gates of hell are worse than the devil has ever known. Lucifer has been frozen out because of his treachery once more..

Amazingly he appeals to God with an aphorism, *"If it ain't broke, don't fix it!"* No response, *"For all time we souls without nerves or brains capable of feeling actual pain have languished in this pit called hell." "Nowhere does it say we've supposed to be cold." "Kindly turn the heat back on."*

The reality of hell is in the loss of connection to God and a communion of other saints. Hell is the sizzle; the alienation from God is the steak. As the temperature of the pit within the earth known as hell decreases, the ambient temperature falls to 55 degrees Fahrenheit. It's tolerable for some but a bit chilly for most.

But to lost souls this change from the extreme is unbearable. They cry out, *"Give us back our fire; this cold is worse."* They finally know the pain of the Lord's cold shoulder. Hell is as cold as is one's dead soul.

A group of insurgents spared from the laser are the clones. While they came to the fray they didn't come with free will. They just were told to be here and bring weapons. Unlike some before who were trained to seek and destroy these were abandoned when an ignoble effort was undertaken by long gone villains.

When hell inherited their masters, Lucifer was stuck with them as well. The whole purpose of this intentionally flawed encirclement and attack was a trick by the devil. He wanted to rid himself of tedious souls and problems. As usual he's whining when his deceptions don't work as he plans. He spouts, *"The clones are not eligible for hell because they've committed no sin."*

Fortunately for these pathetic copies they rarely meet the individuals from whom they're generated anymore. This wasn't the case before when they were targeted by design to replace. They look like their originator did at an early stage of life. When they meet there's little or no sign of recognition. Lucien has a plan. *"We need Mark!"*

Mark and Rosie have settled into their happy stage of post honeymoon bliss. However, Mark has been tasked with finding new and worthy charitable destinations for his company. It's not as easy as it seems. For not all who cry out for alms are worthy as has often been written.

The angels ponder, *"How to make clones fit into a corporate charity?"* Ralph has an idea. A new homeless camp appears before the clones. They are tired and hungry.

No one keeps them away from the tents. *"We will just stop and rest for a while and leave at the first sign of trouble."*

As Lucifer shivers he also chuckles at he has shifted his problems. *"I would be happy if I wasn't so damned and cold!"* *"At least I got rid of Strangler, the creep."* A quivering voice from the far side replies, *"No boss, I'm BACK!"*

Rosie is still working as a military police person. Just after the end of her shift for no particular reason she turns off onto a side road. Just to justify her odd behavior to herself she mutters, *"Maybe I'll find something to wear over at the mall."* She doesn't know if this road leads to the mall, but it might.

She feels slightly less confused. When she starts to pass an obvious homeless encampment on her left she stops. It happens to be on an outlying parcel of the post.

Wearing her uniform and sidearm she appears to the clones to be in her rightful place. They wish her no harm.

And one explains they will be gone immediately if she orders them to do so.

Rosie tells them to stand fast. She will see whether she can learn if anything can be done to improve their plight. Rosie no longer wants to shop. She heads for home.

The games not over for Dumas…

As Dumas begins to think the celestials are toying with his hope for a reward in eternity another familiar phenomenon appears.

The game!

As before these four horse vans pull onto a large parking lot beneath where he hovers. As before they park next to one another lined up exactly. Again from each a white unicorn steps smartly out to the numbered starting point. The silent signal is given. Each beautiful unicorn sets out on its' own way seeking its' best path through an intricate maze. It is up to each unicorn to find the only one to some mysterious exotic wonderful prize at a golden spot in the middle.

With its magnificent horn held proudly high in a stately manner; Dumas sees they are only virtual creatures without matter. Exactly as when he saw them last. The first into this winding maze is blocked and crumbles into dust where it stands. And of course the boohorn shouts. *"Loser!"* Reappearing with its beautiful white mane flowing the refreshed image it trots back into the van it left.

Dumas closes his eyes to make the entire game disappear from his mind. He refuses to allow any part of the game into his thoughts. The gamer shouts something insulting after him. And the boohorn gives him the raspberry. Dumas refuses to listen and has lost his compulsion to ever watch another for the problems of reality are true and games are false.

He looks around as a single engine plane writes his award…DUMAS WINS.

20

Sweet charity

Mark's company truck shows up at the campsite around dawn. The initial alarm the clones feel gives way to joy as the sweet scent of breakfast wafts in the morning breeze through the camp. Mark and a group of coworkers stand smiling ready with a chow line. Meanwhile Rose pushes through a short term emergency camping permit for the group. Mark's about to establish his new corporate charity.

Mark presents his project to the Board. He's too new and was granted so many company shares through his brother Lorenzo's influence no one challenges him, including Lorenzo who wonders where these people came from. But says nothing to chill Mark's enthusiasm. Company records show that a planned lower income subdivision was tabled four years ago.

No one in the area considered themselves to be low income. It was a charitable idea without the needy. Now there are a bunch of these very interesting needies.

A small group of student social workers are on loan from the college social worker student course. And this fits right into their program. Unscathed by bad experiences with fakes and malingerers these young women and a few men are eager to raise the living conditions of these nice clients as much as the corporate program funds are willing to allow. As one young lady puts forth. *"Your money; our time."* Best of all it not only fills a need, but it also feels good.

Dumas, on the other hand has just been rescued by two old friends who are Seraphim angels. The first of Lucien's students, simply called herself Raven. Following Raven was another who we knew as Hawk. The third isn't with them for several reasons. One of which she's finishing her training elsewhere. Secondly, she and Dumas were at odds. She was always just Raven as well.

When Lucifer planned his attack he stipulated Dumas as a target for possible ransom. Everyone in the spiritual dimension knows Dumas to be loved by the very angels who once dubbed him Dumb ass. The Clones couldn't see him to catch him. The rogue robots and devil demons were turned to ash or dust too quickly to avoid these Seraphim as they swept him up and away.

If Dumas or his rescuers had looked down upon Lucien, Roman and Ralph, they would see tears as they loved Dumas. He won't ever return to his home. For the very reason the twins, Mark and Lorenzo were sent off by their parents. The three guardian angels of the hill are too much of a target of retaliation. Revenge from the demons, clone masters and even combat robots is focused upon the *seemingly* most vulnerable. *"Am I going to heaven?"* His rescuers answer matter of factly, *"A heaven more suited for you."* He just sighs.

Rosie asks the military post for an extension of the permit for the clone encampment. It's now a beehive of social activity for social worker college students and those to be rescued from something. Fearing the post will be reduced if congress has the idea there's excess space, they limit the extension to five days and not another.

This gives Mark an opportunity to get his company even more involved in this project. So far they've been involved in supplies and coordination. Not a big expenditure for one of the regional business giants. As

Lorenzo warns Mark, *"The Board will close you out unless you can show something so significant they can use it in our Annual Report."*

Their weekends are consumed with packing lunches and exploring possible places to set up a new campsite for the clones. Mark points out, *"It must be near the college, or their social work becomes difficult."* She agrees. They decide to have the company buy up land from a former family farm. It's about 18 acres and not too far from the school.

The sale is quick without much negotiation except the family insists on using the old family name. This is more of a problem than one might think because the Board insists on using the company name instead. Another meeting and a slight increase in the offer seals the deal.

As the company wants a more formal habitat than mere tents, they bring in tiny houses with almost miniature furnishings. The clones are happy. But are becoming less healthy. Then the shocker. A student comes to the Board and explains these folks have no history. Furthermore, DNA results lead to area families with no knowledge of them.

But that becomes a moot issue when they bring the families to meet their strange biological relations. Lucien feels a bit uneasy with the knowledge that no one has the slightest inkling these are clones. While she feels it's somewhat unethical she knows Lorenzo and Sis must suspect.

The three angels decide not to stir this pot. If Lorenzo and Sis think about it they don't discuss their clones suspicions either. The program is the lesser of evils. And fearing the return of these who are sinless, the devil will never tell.

Crazy as it may seem, the clones don't know. Lorenzo slyly mentions to Mark, *"I think we should get them some form of work with the company so we can give them benefits because increasing the workforce at minimum wage will bring down our average employee costs." "It will look good on the Annual Report but isn't enough to reduce the corporate dividend."* Mark marvels at the way big companies work.

Three strange creatures move toward a celestial destination away from where they started. Two angels and a dog named Dumas travel almost as one. Leaving time and distance they chat and laugh about things past. It's a passage to Dumas's final home.

As their conversation slows they approach a wonderful sound. It's as though every angel has stopped to sing for him. It is the sweet sound of the Seraphim. Then Dumas sees a rainbow. It's welcoming him home. At first it appears to be one solid arch but as they approach it's much more. It's a separate arch of every hue. The first is a very gentle blue.

The two good friends stop and bid him well. He hugs and kisses them, and they no longer dwell. Instead they leave with a tear and goodbye. He knows they love him.

"Goodbye, goodbye, goodbye! "

As Dumas passes beneath the colors of this rainbow he feels the beauty within each. And wonders why he never saw this for it was always within reach. And then he reaches the end. It is the perfect place for Dumas. But it would not be right for one with a human soul. For this heaven is special. And that is where the story of a dog who just wanted to be loved ends.

###

www.ingramcontent.com/pod-product-compliance
Lightning Source LLC
Chambersburg PA
CBHW071258250626
47159CB00004B/1235